Harpoon

MATTHEW WILLIS

CONTENTS

HARPOON

Part One

DAY 0
12 June 1942

It was the day Rommel smashed his way out of The Cauldron. That evening Edmund Clydesdale ascended to the flight deck and one item at a time threw everything he had received from his family over the side. Letters dodged and flipped in the turbulence before the insistence of gravity laid them on the slopping waves. The pen his half-hearted Wren gave him last birthday tumbled lethargically and speared into the surface. The watch from his father flashed with the last light of the sun before the Mediterranean subsumed it.

The emptying of everything he had been continued into the pilots' briefing. The part of his mind that was still alive listened intently, took in each hammerblow phrase. *"Malta only has a week more petrol for its aircraft...only a food for another fortnight...Afrikakorps advancing west at high speed into Egypt...means Malta is now the only base for our aircraft to halt his supplies...if we lose it, the enemy could overrun the entire Med..."* The mission was all that mattered. The rest of him shut down, bit by bit. Dully Edmund absorbed just how bad it was. They had a handful of outdated fighters against two entire air forces, intent on stopping them. The deck sloped under his feet, and it felt like the world was pivoting around this moment.

Soon, in one way or another, all this would end. He went to his camp bed in the Captain's Writer's office. Reborn. Or already dead. As Edmund lay on the canvas, arms folded his behind his head As his eyes closed, he seemed to fall into light.

It was the journalist, Vickery, who pulled him back.

A knock at the door, no pause for an answer, and the Wardroom steward was pushing in, talking rattling, fussing. "Sorry sir, to disturb you, but we had to find a berth for this

1

gentleman, sir, and, well, this was the only place left. Shall I rig up another partition?" He nodded at the canvas screen already set to separate Edmund's 'cabin' from the Captain's Writer's desk.

"There's hardly space," Edmund mumbled, sitting up.

"No sir, quite right sir, I'll just put the bed down here then sir."

"I'm dreadfully sorry about all this," said a voice half out of the passageway behind the bustling steward, who was now assembling a second camp bed like the one Edmund was lying on. Urbane. Older. Dear Lord, were they putting an Admiral in here with him? "I'm told there was nowhere else."

Edmund rubbed his eyes. Not an Admiral. Civilian. "No, I suppose not. Dear old *Eagle* wasn't built for this sort of complement." He half rose and extended his hand. "Sub- er, Acting Le'tenant Clydesdale. Edmund, if you like."

The newcomer took his hand and gave it a brisk shake. "Vickery. Press Association. I'd give you my first name but it's unpronounceable. Everyone just calls me Vickery."

"Pleased to meet you." Edmund hoped he sounded sincere.

"Likewise."

The steward finished assembling the bed and excused himself. Vickery placed his bag on the deck and slid it underneath his bed with one foot.

"I was up on the goofer's earlier watching the sunset. That was you I saw on the flight deck wasn't it?"

Edmund blinked, suddenly uncomfortable, swung his legs off the bed and stood. He was now on a level, give or take half a head, with the journalist and looked at him properly for the first time. Late fifties, perhaps. Face creased, a little weather-beaten but lacking in grog-blossom. Used to smiling but with eyes that suggested there wasn't much to smile about these days. An appearance that spoke of wear and tear, but with an underlying

2

energy. Edmund felt himself similarly appraised, the stranger taking in how short he was for a pilot, his wiry brown hair that would never lie down flat, his no-colour-in-particular eyes...

"It might have been," Edmund said after a moment's silence that stretched too far. "I was up there a little while ago."

"Throwing things over the side?"

Edmund tried hard not to let his teeth clench - or his brow tighten. "Yes. That was me."

Vickery said nothing. Edmund kept his mouth shut. Eventually the journalist nodded. "I've disturbed you. Might I stand you a drink in the wardroom by way of recompense?"

He could hardly refuse, still less tell the old goat to go by himself.

He shrugged, grunted in affirmation and they crossed the passageway to the wardroom. Edmund ignored the drop in the level of conversation as he entered, avoided eye contact, daring some wit or other to remark *snotties and subs in the gunroom!* and found the steward. The armchairs were all occupied so he gestured Vickery to the wardroom table.

Curse the lot of them. He was on the point of freeing himself and they were dragging him back. Edmund's hands tightened on an invisible spade grip, and he forced himself to shake them loose. Hundreds of hours in the air, over Britain, the North Sea, Africa, the Indian Ocean...and now the Mediterranean. Dodging bullets, weather, accidents. All the while chasing a ludicrous goal that had nothing to do with winning the war, that he wanted none of, but chased anyway. He exhaled and realised how tired he was. Like being filled with hot smoke. The thought of closing his eyes and never opening them again...

Vickery's whisky and soda, he noticed, had very little whisky in it. His own had barely a dash. At least he could be proud of that. While others coped by getting thoroughly sozzled, or doped themselves up to the eyeballs on Benzedrine. Not him.

3

He'd got through on his own nerve - single, frayed strand that it now was.

"You weren't aboard before," Edmund said, as the thought occurred to him, "if you only need a berth now. When did you come aboard?"

"A little earlier today. Swordfish flew me from Gib."

"Ah, yes." There had been a floatplane, come to think of it. He'd assumed it was carrying urgent post or dispatches or something like that, or maybe an officer who'd missed the boat.

"You're not a hostilities-only man?" Vickery said after they'd both taken a couple of sips.

"No." Edmund met the reporter's gaze, but could read nothing. How much must he already know? "No, I joined up permanently. It seemed the right thing to do."

"But you weren't intending to be a pilot. Before all this?"

"No." Edmund smiled weakly. Best get it out. Everyone else thought he was an effete little poser, after all. "I had a scholarship to Cambridge. French Literature. Poetry."

To Edmund's surprise, Vickery's eyes sparkled. "Ah, wonderful. I read a bit when I was over there, but never had the time to do it justice. *Demain, dès l'aube, à l'heure où blanchit la   campagne, Je partirai.*" Edmund smiled indulgently - Vickery had a decent accent, but it was a very well-known poem.

Vickery seemed to tuck his genuine pleasure into a corner and was all affable business again. "But for later, perhaps. For now I wonder if I could ask about some aspects of the flying? You needn't worry about presenting it for the layman, I flew in the last war. France. RNAS then RAF. And I've covered rather a lot of flying over the last few years." The questions continued. Flying, yes, then the inevitable 'human interest' stuff that seemed to embarrass Vickery almost as much as it did Edmund. Yes, both parents were alive. No, he was no relation to the Wing

Commander Clydesdale who flew over Everest in '33. Yes, he had a sweetheart - well, if you counted a rather demanding Wren who seemed more interested in showing off her boyfriend (*"he's very nearly an ace, you know!"*) at parties than in the boyfriend himself...

"Aha, Vickery! You found Clydesdale then! Good, good," boomed out behind them. Edmund looked round, half-rose in his chair before being waved back down. It was the Commander Flying, Leake. The ship's PR officer, Lieutenant Ashley was hovering behind, wringing his slender hands.

Vickery smiled, only slightly awkward. "I did indeed, Commander. Thank you."

"There's your story. Top scoring pilot on the ship. You're about due for that promotion to Le'tenant to be made permanent now aren't you Clydesdale? We'll make it happen, don't you worry. And a gong too, I shouldn't wonder."

Clydesdale's mouth hinged open and shut once or twice, without any sound or air going out, but the Commander Flying had already turned back to Vickery.

"He'll make ace tomorrow, sure as eggs is eggs. That's if the Eyeties don't scarper at the sight of us. But I doubt it. They'll send their aircraft in droves, to justify keeping their fleet skulking in harbour."

"I heard there were some signs of cruisers coming out," Vickery replied softly. Not as a question.

"I don't think-" said Ashley.

"Oh, they pop their heads out now and again but invariably pull 'em straight back in," Leake said. "Send their air force to do their dirty work. Mind you, even they turn tail and run at the first sign of opposition. But this lad Clydesdale has a habit of being in the right place to knock 'em down. It's a talent."

A sickening warmth washed through Edmund's ears and began to spread to his neck, jaw, the sides of his face. The

Commander Flying had not even looked at him. But the wardroom had quietened and everyone was looking his way. All those pre-war officers who resented their friendly Swordfish crews being booted ashore in favour of a pack of fighter boys. They regarded Edmund as unquestionably the worst, the most vulgar of the bunch. He hunched over the table.

"There's something about the fellows who get the scores, I tell you," Leake added, though Vickery had asked for no more. "Something different. Extra."

Ashley wrung his hands some more. "Well, all of our pilots-"

Vickery seemed to sense Edmund's mortification. "Isn't a lot of it just luck though? Right place, right time? Not to denigrate anyone's skill, of course. But what I mean to say is, it's possible to be a fine combat pilot and not have many..." He cleared his throat lightly. "Kills?"

For a moment, Edmund thought the Commander Flying was going to seize Vickery by the lapels and shake him. Vickery didn't move, and maintained his placid smile.

"Luck! *Pshaw*. Luck. I ask you. No, it may appear to be luck to the *outsider*." Leake smirked a little. He obviously knew nothing of Vickery's background. "But the really top pilots can sniff out the kills. Make sure they're on the right missions, in the right position. They'll probably see the enemy first - and do everything they can to get at 'em, come what may. No, you mark my words, the chaps who have the highest scores are special."

Leake boomed on, Ashley fluttering away behind him, adding a few tentative qualifications when he could, but Edmund heard little of what was said. He felt the eyes of everyone in the wardroom boring into him. Felt the agonising silence over the scratching gramophone. He took as long over his drink as he could stomach and made his apologies. He lay on the bed listening to the wardroom door opening and closing. Soon it seemed everyone had left or turned in, and there was nothing to hear but the thrum of the turbines. He realised how much tension had built up in his legs, arms, neck, and tried to release it. But then another voice cut across the passageway.

"Wouldn't listen to a bloody word Old Leaky says. He flew Flycatchers in the twenties. Jolly-jolly-what-ho flying club stuff, and he thinks it's all still like that. Let me tell you about the fellows who 'get the scores'. To a man they are murderous arseholes. Utter scum you wouldn't waste your saliva to spit on in civvy life."

Who was that? Lewis-Evans?

"Whenever I find I've got someone like that on my squadron, I do what I can to get rid of them."

Yes, that was him. Who was he talking to? A more even voice replied.

"Alright, so the real aces can be a bit...intense. But that's just because they're so focussed. Aren't they the ones winning the war?"

Of course, Vickery, the journalist. He was supposed to be crimping here with Edmund, so of course he hadn't crashed out yet.

Lewis-Evans snorted. "Are they, bollocks. When a chap is so concerned about his tally, he doesn't give a tuppenny toss about the lives of the other pilots or the mission or the war, for that matter. All that matters to him is scratching another swastika by the cockpit."

"But if he's shooting down the enemy..."

"If shooting down the enemy was the only thing we had to do, that would be wonderful, but it isn't. In our line, knocking down the odd Jay-You Eighty-Eight is neither here nor there. Jerry's got thousands of the bloody things, he won't miss a handful. Even the Skipper's only got two, give or take the odd probable, and he could have had half a dozen more if that was all he cared

7

about. You're not telling me that little squit Clydesdale is a better pilot than the Skipper. No, what we can do best, what we should be doing, is breaking up raids. Messing up their aim. Getting them to turn around, ditch their bombs early, get the blazes away. The war won't be won out here, but it could be lost. This little jaunt, Operation 'Harpoon', is the first time we've given a Malta convoy any kind of air cover worth the name, but we're too few to piss around destroying individual crates, never mind fiddling about confirming them."

"It's good for morale back home, though. To see fellows being successful in the air."

Lewis-Evans laughed, a metallic, inhuman sound. "We can make up whatever heroics we like to put a bit of backbone into the good folk of dear old Blighty. Most of the stuff they're told is fantasy anyway. Might as well be all of it. I don't know why we don't just tell fellows like you any old thing. One of our clapped out Hurribangers knocked down thirty of their Ess-Emm Seventy-Nines, then pressed on to Rome to shove a two hundred and fifty pounder up Mussolini's arsepipe."

A hollow chuckle. "Well, that would be an easy sell to my editor. But I'm afraid I prefer things to have the ring of truth."

"Truth! Ha. Whatever next?"

There was a silence. Edmund could have laughed. Some would have taken it as shock at Lewis-Evans' words, but he'd seen Vickery in action. That shabby old journalist's trick, leave a space open for your victim to fall into. People do hate silence, don't they? Lewis-Evans wasn't dense enough to fall for it though. Surely.

"See those bastards coming down after a kill, though," the Senior Pilot went on. "See them get out of their machines, like the world isn't big enough to contain them. Like they've done something that's...I don't know, beyond the human. And I suppose they have, haven't they? They've *killed*. How do you think it would be if...if...to be a bloody good dancer, or a footballer or something, to really excel at it...someone else had to die. Would people really go for it? I bet some of them bloody would."

Another pause seeped out of the wardroom. And then: "I bet that bastard Clydesdale would."

Lewis-Evans, or possibly Vickery, must have realised the door was open at that moment, for there were footsteps and then the click of the latch. He still caught the following words: "Can't understand it, you know. His flying is average and in training his shooting was piss-poor". Edmund lay in the half-darkness. His mind had turned to concrete. There was nothing left. If he had managed a kill tomorrow, or the day after - a proper one, that he had earned, perhaps that would have been something. But now it only proved...what, exactly? He felt ludicrously awake. Dog-tired but awake, left leg full of twitch and damn it now the right one was joining in. And his back throbbed, thanks to this bloody bed. Sleep was impossible. He knew he'd be lying here when morning came, and yet he must have slept as the clack of the door brought him back to the moment. Vickery was standing in the doorway.

"Sorry," the journalist whispered, "didn't mean to wake you."

"You could hardly not have in this cupboard," Edmund slurred. "By which I mean it's alright. Don't worry about it."

Vickery chuckled. "Thank you." He began to undress and in a few moments creaked into his own bed.

Edmund lay on his back, staring at the deck above. He wanted to roll onto his side, away from Vickery, but did not do so, and idly wondered why. Was this the same sort of paralysis that had sometimes grabbed him in combat? Was there something fundamentally lethargic about him? While he wondered, he listened to Vickery's breathing. It was even. But it was not the breathing of a man asleep.

"I wonder if you heard any of that conversation with your Senior Pilot earlier," Vickery said. The words sliced across the gloom. Edmund winced as they struck.

"Enough of it," he said. "It's alright. I know what they think of me."

Vickery said nothing for a moment, but there was an awkwardness in the creak of his camp bed just then. "I don't suppose they mean it. It's not an easy business, as you know. Your Splot has only one kill himself, I gather."

"You heard him. He doesn't care about the kills."

"No, and I believe he's right not to. But when everyone else goes on about it so. It can't be easy to hear the kind of thing the Commander Flying was saying earlier."

"No. Yes. Well it wasn't all that easy for me to hear, frankly."

"I don't suppose for a moment that it was."

"I don't bloody go on about it!" Edmund hissed. "I wish everyone else would shut up. I feel the same way they do. Rommel's just broken out and started breezing through Egypt, capturing all the airfields and ports. We're on the brink of losing the eastern Med altogether and all they can talk about is... Bloody *cricket* scores! I didn't set out..."

For an instant, urgent as heartburn, Edmund's need to pour out the whole sorry story boiled through him. The confession of his fraud. That he'd lucked into four kills that had brought him to the brink of being an ace. The sheer idiocy of it all. He imagined the papers at home. He'd be famous as a kind of clown. Like Old Mother Riley, defeating the Nazis through ineptitude. It was bloody hilarious. He tried to smother a chuckle and failed.

"Care to share the joke, Acting Lieutenant?"

"Not really." *I'm the joke!* he wanted to scream. *I'm the bloody joke! I'll go up there tomorrow and the Eyeties and Jerries will probably piss themselves to see the way I fly. I'll have a crack anyway, be blown to atoms and the Navy's press people will say 'what a pity he didn't get one more before he carked it' and move on to the next poor bastard.* "It's nothing."

"You got your first with the RAF didn't you?"

Oh, oh, Mr Reporter's going to keep on prodding until he gets something worthwhile. Edmund sighed. "Yes. They were asking for volunteers after France. Everyone on my course volunteered, so I did too. Got sent to Nineteen Squadron. On Spits. First sortie was on Battle of Britain Day, would you believe? I got a One-One-Oh."

"First time out, eh? Impressive."

"It just happened, really."

"The training does kick in when the time comes, doesn't it?"

That time Edmund let himself laugh. A sharp-edged cackle that filled the tiny space. "I'll tell you about it, shall I?"

First kill

15 September 1940

Combat report Acting Pilot Officer E.G. Clydesdale.

"…Squadron was climbing to intercept point when bounced by 15-20 Messerschmitt Me110 over Swanley. After initial pass, engagement turned into a generalised dogfight. I was able to manoeuvre on the tail of a 110 and slightly below, and opened fire at a distance of approximately 150 yards. It was easy to stay on E/A's tail and I was able to fire one short and one long burst at close range, seeing gunfire striking the E/A around the centre-section and cockpit. No return fire was observed. E/A caught fire, flipped over and fell away in an inverted spin trailing smoke. No parachutes observed."

***

The Spitfires were climbing into a clear sky. Edmund glanced to each side, making sure he was precisely equidistant from the Squadron Leader to his left - to port - and Blue Three. First mission. His heart was surging, rattling off his ribcage. First mission. There was a bag of Dorniers a few miles away. Would he get one? The sun flashed off Blue Leader's canopy. It was hard to believe there was a war-

In that instant the equilibrium of the climb shattered. Radio silence flipped to a cacophony of voices fizzing through the airwaves. What? Had anyone said 'break?' Dimly, Edmund knew they were under attack. He knew he should do something. Probably break, but... He looked out for his flight leader. Gone. He should do something. His hands seemed frozen on the controls. Break. But which way? He tried to tune his hearing into the radio. Maybe Blue Leader was calling him... *Geoff, break right!...on my tail...bail out Dobbs, bail out...God's sake...confirm your angels, I repeat...* The Spitfire climbed on, flying straight. The sky ahead was the same, apart from a strange, flickering series of stripes darting by the wings. Like unfurling streamers thrown from behind.

Oh Jesus. Tracers.

Break.

Break.

His hands were immobile, clamped to the spade grip. Any second now he would move them. Any moment now.

A shadow flickered across him and in that moment, filling the canopy above, impossible, huge, wallowing, a Messerschmitt One-One-Oh. Close enough that he could have read the stencils, if he understood German. The moment was filled, blown out merely with the wonder of that sight. The streaks of staining behind the exhausts, the landing flaps lowered...and there *puff!*

puff! two jets of smoke that meant the throttles had been opened wide.

The One-One-Oh was barely drawing ahead and sagging down in front of him. Dimly, somewhere in the fog filling Edmund's skull, a voice told him, conversationally, *silly bugger's overshot, tried to slow himself down, now he's in a pickle all right*. He almost felt sorry for the German as he let his thumb fall softly onto the button, felt the brassy clunk as it triggered, the muffled hammering of the eight Brownings. The shock of it lifted his thumb involuntarily, but then he was mashing it again onto the button, and the tracers were blasting out of his wings, into the Messerschmitt. He didn't even need to aim. It was almost disappointing. A constellation erupted around the wingroots, the cockpit. *Stupid bastard! Stupid bastard! Make a mistake like that and you deserve to buy it!* He kept his thumb down until nothing but air was rushing through the guns. It was enough. A flare of white flame in the midst of the Messerschmitt, a buttery streak of smoke - and the thing had flipped onto its back. As Edmund finally remembered to put his Spitfire's nose down and open the throttle wide, the Messerschmitt simply fell out of the sky.

***

12 June 1942

Edmund stared straight up towards the deck above, his vision consumed in the darkness before reaching the painted metal. The sound of his voice recounting the story followed it into nothingness. Why in heaven's name had he phrased it like that? "Was able to manoeuvre on the tail of a 110..." Well yes, he was on the tail of the 110, and he was able to manoeuvre... But he'd made it sound as though he did it on purpose...that he'd found a 110 and chased it. Why on earth hadn't he just written it as it had happened? If there'd been any justice no-one would have seen and it wouldn't have been confirmed, but of course they were over Kent and the smashed-up Jerry was easy to confirm. A couple of other 19 Squadron pilots had even seen him, apparently calmly blasting a Messer out of the sky at point-blank range. Good Lord. What a mess.

"I don't know if it was that," Edmund said eventually. "Reflexes, perhaps. But as you said to Leake. Right place, right time. Luck. Just luck." Luck that the pilot had chopped his throttles, stuck his flaps down trying to stay behind Edmund's Spit. And, having done so, had virtually no control authority until the engines picked up, and could do nothing but sit there. It was clear as day, clear as the air at thirty thousand. A child could have got that kill, had one found themselves in Edmund's cockpit at that moment. A monkey. A well-trained dog.

"Well, you say that..." Vickery didn't sound too convinced. Well what did he know, anyway?

"It was. We were bounced. I was lucky. Extremely lucky. If things had gone even a tiny bit differently, it would have been me blown out of the sky instead of that Jerry." If there was any justice...

"What was it Napoleon said?"

"'Not tonight, Josephine?'"

Vickery laughed. "Possibly. But I was thinking more of preferring lucky generals to good ones."

"Oh. I can understand that, I think."

"There's another comment attributed to him, though, which may be loosely translated as 'you make your own luck'."

"That, if you'll pardon my saying so, is rot."

"Quite possibly. And yet life has a way of following rules that seem to be ridiculous."

"Yes. It does." Rules like him being the carrier's top scoring pilot, when he was almost certainly its worst. Luck. It wasn't all it was cracked up to be. Edmund turned on his side, but sleep was more elusive than ever. Every noise and movement jolted him further into wakefulness. Well he needn't worry about being too deadly to the enemy tomorrow. Although he'd probably nod off in the cockpit and still manage to shoot something down in his sleep. He snorted with amusement.

"Still awake then?" Vickery said.

"Yes," Edmund replied, teeth gritted.

"Sorry." There was a sound of Vickery shifting his position on a canvas bed. "I just wanted to say that one victory might be put down to luck, but you've had four."

Edmund laughed again, but it came out like a sob. "Everybody says that. That's rot, too. Listen to me." He turned over to face Vickery, even though he could barely see the man. "Luck is luck. You toss a coin, it can be heads or tails. Every single time it's 50-50. You're just as likely to throw a hundred heads or a hundred tails as half-and-half."

"Well technically..."

"Technically means 'how things work'. You can be lucky in the air every single time. Skill, ability, judgement... Doesn't come into it."

"I'm sure a lot of chaps feel that way."

"I'm telling you." Edmund wanted to scream it. He felt his fists clenching, arms tensing. He exhaled, forcing himself to calm down. "It's possible to be lucky - not just a bit fortunate, I mean blind, beat-the-house lucky time in, time out. Think about it. Statistically, one or two people could just get the right result every time they tried something. Couldn't they?"

"Hmm." Edmund was unconvinced. "Anyway," he went on, trying to hold back the reckless urge, failing. "Luck isn't just in the air. It's not even though all of my kills were even mine."

"Oh?"

Edmund could hear Vickery's sense of decency warring with his curiosity. How deeply the journalist wanted to say something reassuring. And how viscerally he wanted to shut up and give Edmund enough rope to hang himself. Vickery took a breath, but Edmund leapt in anyway.

"My second kill."

"Oh. Yes. You were back with the Fleet Air Arm by that stage, weren't you?"

"Yes. I came back in December '40 and was posted to Eight-Oh-One. Worked up on the Sea Hurricane, then went North. Remember the Petsamo-Kirkenes fiasco?"

"I heard of it, yes. Bit of a massacre."

"I'll say. Not that I was involved in that side of it, we were just protecting the ships while the Applecores and Fulmars went to get a pasting over the fjords. In fact, we didn't see much until we were on the way home. A Dee-Oh Eighteen shadower latched onto us."

Second kill
31 July 1941

Combat report Midshipman E.G. Clydesdale RNVR, 801 Squadron HMS *Furious*. Sea Hurricane IB 'R'

"Alert fighter scrambled for interception of shadower as wingman to Squadron Commander, two-aircraft element. Directed by RDF, Dornier Do18 sighted ten miles distant from fleet at zero feet, heading east. Commenced with head-on attack, then proceeded to make quarter attacks, scoring some hits. Ordered to take lead by Flight Leader, following his guns jamming. On the fourth attack, E/A abruptly departed from controlled flight and crashed into the sea. No dinghies or men in the water observed. Too low for parachutes."

***

"Bogey turning zero-eight-five, angels two, your new bearing for intercept zero-one-zero."

Joyce acknowledged and banked to starboard. Edmund stayed on his quarter. For a while, all was quiet, still. Then Joyce began to descend, and Edmund fought a frantic need to start adjusting throttle and trim to stay in position. This was close enough.

"Close up, Green Two," fizzed through the phones. "On the deck so he doesn't see us."

"Yes, Green Leader," he said, desperate not to shriek with the tension.

"Do you see him?"

The span of Edmund's focus had encompassed only Joyce's wingtip and the caps of the waves below; now barely below. "No, Green Leader." He allowed a second, two seconds looking ahead, scanning from side to side. Nothing.

"Ten o'clock?"

Ten o'clock. Nothing. Just grey sky, wisps of darker torn-rag billowing across. And then. Something, seen as an irritation in his vision. Like a misplaced hyphen on a page, a black dash skimming over the wavetops. Already a memory as his eyes slipped off it. But no, there was the irritation again. "Got it, Green Leader."

"About bloody time. I'm going to work around head-on first, then swing back for a quarter attack. First pass, I'll fire then pull to starboard to let you have a pop, but you'll have to be quick about it. Stay close but not too close."

"OK Green Leader."

There would hardly be any time. Edmund checked his guns were armed again. Joyce was banking, his wingtip almost carving a furrow in the sea, and Edmund let his Hurricane float upwards slightly. There was the dash directly ahead, and in a moment the shape of an aeroplane appeared. And oh God Joyce was moving aside - and he was hardly lined up and his thumb hit the button, but his tracers went high. A huge black cross was momentarily silhouetted against the sky and they were past. He fell in behind Joyce and followed the other Hurricane into a wingover.

"Bloody guns jammed!" Joyce hissed out of his headphones. "All bloody eight! Barely fired a round. Can't get the bloody things to work." There was a sound of breathing like the sea through the R/T. "*You* missed by a bloody mile."

"Yes, Green Leader."

"Right. You take the lead Green Two. This is your job now. Remember, driving him off is the main thing, but if we down him, he can't make any report at all."

Right. His lead. Right. Christ. A quarter attack. That was what Joyce had said. If he messed up the approach it would end in a stern chase and that was the best way of getting a face-full of 20mm cannon fire. Alright...gain a bit of height to give the overspeed. There was the enemy...a Dornier flying boat, exactly the same colour as the sea. Hard to see where it ended and the waves began. Their courses would intersect some way ahead. He'd done this in training with a drogue, but somehow this was totally different. Finally, he had to commit, put the nose down a touch. He felt the Hurricane picking up speed. Immediately he knew he'd overdone it and would cross some way ahead of the Dornier if he maintained course. He started to edge back to port with a tweak of rudder, of aileron, but it was almost a beam attack now and they were converging too quickly. The Hurricane balked at the control input and for a second wanted to bunt. When he'd coaxed it back the flying boat already filled the canopy but instinctively he remembered to fire...the tracers seemed to be going in roughly the right direction this time but in a flash he was past.

"Balls," Joyce rasped. "Too much bloody deflection. Did you forget the nose drops if you use too much rudder?" For a second Edmund thought there was interference on the R/T but it was just Joyce sighing. "Turn...starboard nine-zero, try again."

He thought he'd got it right this time but again found himself overshooting, tried to switch to a curving approach in the last few hundred yards which helped. But still the Dornier was only in his sights for a fraction of a second, time for the shortest of bursts. As they flicked past, the flying boat was still skimming serenely on its way.

"I think you probably hit him that time." Joyce's irritation was clear even through the hissing and popping of the radio. "Once or twice. But at this rate you'll be out of ammo before we do him any damage. He's turning into the attacks each time, do you see?"

Of course. That's why the approach kept getting messed up in the last part. How to account for it? The drogue never turned in. "Yes, Green Leader. Are your guns still jammed?"

"Tighter than a debutant's fanny. Alright, let's split up. I'll make a mock attack from starboard, and you aim to come in from port a moment after." Joyce's Hurricane sheered away and Edmund watched it arcing out, S-turning back. This time it was easier to judge - as the Dornier tried to turn in towards Joyce's attack. He had a moment longer to line up, a moment longer with his tracers playing on the wing.

"Again," Joyce ordered. It seemed to play out as before but Joyce held on until he was much closer, much less than a hundred yards, and as he broke away in front of the Dornier. As Edmund began to fire, the flying boat reared, nose in the air. The black slab of the Dornier filled his windscreen and he whipped the Hurricane into a turn, the airframe bouncing and creaking with protest and for a moment he thought he'd overdone it. When the Hurricane was back on an even keel, he banked to starboard...the Dornier was gone. He tightened the turn. A patch of white foam marred the surface...and there, the triple tail of the Dornier sliding nauseatingly into the waves and out of sight.

"You got him! You got him!" cut through the static in his headphones. "Bloody good shooting, Clydesdale!"

"Thank you, Green Leader." The words came out automatically but Edmund wasn't sure how he'd said them. What the hell had just happened?

Jesus. The Dornier stalled in. Just stalled in. The pilot had probably reacted to Joyce's Hurricane almost colliding with him and manoeuvred too hard. Edmund spluttered. "He...just..."

"Repeat please Green Two?"

"He just went in. Straight in."

"Good show, you probably hit the elevator controls."

"I...Yes. Perhaps."

"All right. Return to *Furious*. Good show, Clydesdale."

"Yes sir. Thank you, sir."

***

12 June 1942

This time, of course, he hadn't embellished the report at all, and hadn't even stated explicitly that he'd shot the aircraft down. But then he hadn't added his belief that the Dornier had simply stalled in and crashed either. Not when Joyce had been so full of praise. It had been good to hear, hadn't it? Even when he knew it was nonsense, that if anything the kill should be credited to Joyce?

And even now, he found himself hedging as he described the encounter to Vickery. He might not want all this, Edmund told himself, but neither did he want to be plastered all over the dailies as a comic turn. *The Accidental Ace*, perhaps. *Edmund The Unworthy*. Or *The Phoney Fighter Boy...*

"You aren't going to write about any of this are you?" he said to Vickery when he'd finished the story of his second victory.

"Of this conversation? No, of course not! You have my word. I have to run anything I write past Lieutenant Ashley anyway."

"No, I mean about any of it. About me. About the bloody kills."

"I can't very well avoid it, I'm afraid. The Admiralty will insist. But I promise you it will be sympathetic."

"If you mean you'll make me look good, I don't want that either! I don't want to be added to some glorious list of heroes." Christ. The whole business was spiralling out of control. He pictured the fictitious version of himself. The one that would be presented to the public. Square of jaw, skilful of hand. A fantasy Edmund Clydesdale who, when he was gone, would supplant the real one. It was already supplanting the real one. He felt himself begin to evaporate next to the radiance of the hero, Edmund Clydesdale. The Ace.

"Mm-hmm. I do remember this. Very well. And I'm sorry," Vickery said softly, his voice full of solidarity. "It's a difficult enough job to do without worrying about how it all looks to the outside, what your comrades will make of it and so on. Believe me, I've little enough interest in stories of individual heroism packaged up by our lords and masters to stiffen resolve on 'Civvie Street'. There are enough genuine cases like that to fill volumes. I know you're no aerial Achilles, for goodness sake. No, I see well enough that fellows like you are just ordinary chaps doing your best to grapple with the monumental task that's been placed in your hands. But isn't that enough?"

Edmund exhaled. "That's all, really. If the convoy gets through, who cares how it happens?"

"Quite." There was a pause, a moment in which the turbines could be heard, the torpid roll of the hull felt. "Preferably with the minimum of loss of life."

Edmund could have laughed. The minimum. There could not be none. So, let the minimum be one. He would chase that fifth victory into the jaws of Hell, and then this would be over, one way or another. They'd left him no choice. "Well I suppose."

The bed opposite creaked and Edmund supposed Vickery had sat up. "Your chances are good, though, I imagine."

Edmund smiled to himself. "Sooner or later one's luck has to run out."

"I mean to say...you do *want* to..."

"Get my fifth? Of course. Who wouldn't?"

"That wasn't...er..."

Just bloody say it, man. No, for God's sake don't bloody say it. "Wasn't what?" Edmund asked, his voice all beatific innocence.

"Ah, nothing," the older man said, his voice a rasp against the soft darkness. "It doesn't matter. I just meant it's better to live to fight another day if you can."

"Yes, of course." Another day. Another whole day. And then another, and another. The idea was ludicrous, intolerable. He should walk out of the office, up to the flight deck and just keep walking. He had stripped himself away and they had bound his self back to him. He had broken free from the ball and chain of himself, resolved to become Clydesdale the Ace, even if doing so dragged him below anyway.

"Well, good night," he said, slicing off what might have remained of the conversation.

"Good night," Vickery replied, his voice thin, desolate. "Sleep well."

Edmund lay awake, thoughts unable to settle on anything, running away after one memory and abruptly switching to another. Kent, 1940... The North Sea, 1941... Egypt 1942... the third kill... Just as he'd given up hope of any rest at all, he fell into oblivion, and dreamed he was lost in muffling fog, which stuffed his throat when he tried to shout. He then felt himself falling, with no parachute, down, down...

DAY 1
13 June 1942

Edmund opened his eyes. There was activity outside, enough that it had tipped the delicate balance of sleep. Footsteps padded by in the passageway outside. The Middle Watch had given way to the Morning Watch. The tone of the engines had whirred up, and the deckhead started vibrating above him. A flake of paint landed on his forehead. HMS *Eagle* was waking from her half-doze, to become a warship once more, alert and aggressive. Within a few hours he would be in the air again.

Something he had realised long ago it hit him now with the full force of gravity, vertically from ten thousand feet, and alone, in the dark, with all his defences and justifications stripped away. There was nothing to protect him from what he had done.

That third kill. That was not his at all. And he had killed his wingman in getting it.

Not just a liar, not just a fraud. A murderer.

Christ. He felt the sweat on his palms again. This time it was cold.

The official notification had Leonard down as missing, of course. And at the time, Edmund had believed it had been an accident, a tragic mistake. Now, though, it had seemed so obvious he didn't know how anyone could have concluded differently.

Jesus.

He had to put it right. He had to put all this right. But how? How did you put something like this back together? If he died, what did it serve?

Justice, the answer came back. Justice. But what was personal, individual justice when there was a war to win? Wasn't there a greater justice?

He could not unpick whether that reasoning was cowardice or courage. Like an Escher sketch, it could be either depending on how you looked at it. He felt stinging, frustrated tears joining the sweat leaking out of him and wondered if there was any salt left in his body. And with it, over the last few days, weeks, something else seemed to be leaving him. Courage, perhaps? Or willpower?

It was only then that he noticed Vickery's bed was empty. For a moment's panic, like vertigo, he wondered if the journalist had ever existed. But of course he had, or why was there another bed in the office?

There would be no more sleep. Edmund cleaned himself up, dressed, remembered to strap the Omega beacon watch onto his wrist, went to the heads, to the mess and forced some breakfast down, to the heads again. He sat on the thunderbox, staring at the aircraft identification cards pinned to the back of the door. There were a dozen of them, two thirds being types he'd never seen before. The sun was not yet up but when he found his way to the goofers' the day had signalled its intent to start. Vickery was there. Of course he was. Edmund wanted to ask if he was real. Of course he was, and yet perhaps there was more to him. Perhaps he was a harbinger more than a messenger. Things felt different now.

"Morning," the journalist said, as if he were not in the slightest bit surprised to see him up here, even though nothing would be happening on the flight deck for at least half an hour.

"Morning," he replied, thinking of nothing else to say, and turned his gaze to the horizon.

"Will you have a pilots' briefing later?" Vickery asked.

"No. We did that yesterday evening. For the whole convoy. Everyone knows what they have to do."

"I see. Good, good. Keeps things simple."

"Yes."

They lapsed into silence, and Edmund let his mind empty, and the wash of the waves along the hull fill his consciousness for a while.

The aft lift began to lower with a shrill whine ready to bring up the first fighter, throwing the weight of the day to come back at him like a bulkhead had breached. "It'll get rather windy up here at times," he said to Vickery, grasping at anything to hold the mass of it away. "Every time aircraft are flown off and landed on, we'll have to turn west, into wind, and steam at full pelt. And then steam back at full pelt to catch the convoy again." He patted the railing. "The old girl's going to get a bit of exercise today. Hope her creaking joints can manage."

"Old?" Vickery intoned, theatrical offence contorting his features. "Launched 1918, and you call her old? Your own ship! She's not old, she's in her prime!"

"Sorry Vickery," Edmund grinned. "Can you ever forgive me?"

"It's *Eagle* you need to apologise to."

"Quite right." Edmund patted the railing again. "Sorry, old girl."

Vickery shook his head and rolled his eyes heavenward.

"Just so you're aware," Edmund went on, for the sake of anything to say, anything at all, "the aim is to put up a section of two Sea Hurricanes up to patrol every hour. If and when the raids start to come in, more sections will be sent up to reinforce."

"How many aircraft will be up at any one time?" Vickery asked, a slight frown of calculation folding his brow.

"There'll be seven sections overall. Six from Eight-Oh-One Squadron and one from Eight-One-Three's fighter flight. The most we'll be able to maintain in the air is three sections, I'd say. That's the high patrol. There'll be a couple of Fulmars low down too. *Argus* will be operating the Fulmars and the anti-sub Swordfish." He gestured at the wallowing, high-sided, islandless strangeness of the other old carrier already struggling to keep up with the escort.

Vickery nodded slowly, three, four times. "That doesn't seem very many. The Germans and Italians have, what is it, four-hundred and fifty aeroplanes in this sector?"

Edmund shrugged. "Something like that."

The door opened and another pilot emerged. Crosley, one of the four 813 Squadron Hurricane pilots, flustering with excitement. "Oh, hello Clyde," he said. "Tricky says there's a shadower up already! Sixteen miles ahead of the convoy. I dare say we'll see some sport today, eh? Leave some for the rest of us, there's a good chap." He disappeared, vibrating with energy no doubt until he bumped into the next person to tell.

So. It was happening, then. "Alright, I'd better be going," Edmund said eventually. He held out his hand. "I'll say goodbye, just in case."

"Farewell" Vickery smiled, a genuine, face-crinkling expression. "And for want of a better term, good hunting."

Edmund smiled wanly and hurried for the aircrew locker room. At 0730 he was in his flying kit and waiting, although he wasn't scheduled to fly in the early patrols. Edmund checked the roster again. 'Wings' had no doubt seen to it that he would be up later in the day, when there was a better chance of contacts. He traced a finger down the chart and rolled his eyes. Yellow section with Temporary Sub Lieutenant (A) Yeates.

Yellow. It might be a coincidence, of course. Perhaps luck also had a sense of irony. There wasn't a white feather pinned next to his name, after all. Small mercies. He considered heading for the goofers' but then remembered that Vickery would still be there, and he was not ready for that conversation to continue yet. His defences would not last forever. There was a small pilots' crew room in the island, between the funnels, so he went there.

The convoy was still at extreme range for bombers from Italy, and not much better from Sardinia. There were the shadowers, though. Nasty little snoopers hanging around out of AA range and radioing their position to submarines, and darting away as soon as fighters were scrambled, only to pop up again later. As he waited his turn, Edmund pictured a map room somewhere in the Italian Admiralty, their position and strength constantly marked and updated. At least with Sea Hurricanes they had half a chance, but how much better if they'd had the latest mark than their clapped-out Battle of Britain relic Mark Ones? More power, better armament. Even the borrowed RAF machine he'd flown back in Egypt had been better than these crates.

The day was finally here when he could put the past behind him and just fly, just fight. And yet it stretched away endlessly ahead of him. He wouldn't even be in the cockpit until after 1100, and when might the serious attacks start? Probably not until late afternoon. It was tomorrow that would be the real crucible. But tomorrow was an age away. Restlessness charged his muscles with unenergy. It could not rouse him fully, nor would it let him relax. He left the crew room, prowled through the maze of passages, ending up back at his 'cabin'. The Captain's Writer was in there, hammering at his typewriter, so Edmund went to the wardroom and found an armchair. Despite the nervousness fizzing through every blood vessel, unrest finally caught up with him and he fell into a doze almost immediately, only to be woken by the pipe calling *Special Dutymen To Your Stations* as it whistled through the tannoy. The wardroom emptied of officers, and by the time Edmund departed, the surgeon and his assistants were setting up the sick bay in the space left.

Even then, it was wait, wait, wait. Yellow Section would be the fifth in the air. Unless there were large raids reported - not likely this morning - he wouldn't be flying until... Ten, eleven, twelve... thirteen-hundred hours. He was tired, and the day hadn't started. He relented and went up to the goofer's which, by now, was packed, thank Christ. Vickery nodded, but left him alone. The breeze off the Mediterranean, accelerated by 18 knots of *Eagle*'s forward motion, was a balm.

Red section were readied. The CO, Brabner, and Hutton lined up and each ran up their engines. Then Brabner opened-up, the tail of his Hurricane lifting off the deck in the propwash, before he released the brakes and bounded forward. By the time he was level with the island there was already thirty feet of air under the wheels, and Hutton had opened his throttle wide. The two Hurricanes climbed into the waiting sky, receding in the blue-white, heading for their patrol altitude, twelve thousand. Hard to believe with the sun already beginning to heat the exposed metal too hot to touch, but it would be cold up there.

Then Pink section was on standby. Crosley and Spike's Hurricanes were on deck, waiting for an alert. Edmund didn't envy them. It would be hot and uncomfortable in the cockpit, with nothing to do and nothing to take the mind off it. He noticed the other pilots on the gallery studiously ignoring him. Well, that was alright. He pushed his way along to Vickery. It was churlish to avoid the man. The journalist smiled and turned back to the scene on deck. They stood in companionable silence until it was Pink's time to take over the patrol. The two Hurricanes launched, and within a few minutes, Edmund spotted the Red Section planes entering the circuit. He pointed them out to Vickery, who thanked him, though Edmund had a sneaking suspicion the reporter had already seen them. The Hurricanes curved round, keeping the deck in view past the nose, until the last moment of straightening out, then thwack, squeal, thunk down on the deck and restrained by a wire.

Brown Section, then Green, and only then would Yellow be flying. Just before Green were due to launch, at a quarter to twelve, Edmund picked up the paraphernalia all pilots had been given - Italian money, yellow dye, revolver - and went down to the hangar where the kite he'd been assigned ('F' - another coincidence?) was being readied. "I hear Pink got vectored onto a snooper," his rigger, Mac, said as he was secured into the cockpit. "Junkers, they reckon." He pronounced it *joon-kers*.

"Oh," was all he could think to say. "Did they get it?"

"Nah. Buggered off as soon as the Hurris turned up. Chased him for a bit, but, you know... You'll have more luck, sir, I know you will." The rating grinned with genuine pride and Edmund flushed. He exchanged a couple more words with Mac, but neither of them were much in the mood for chat. There had been too much anticipation, not enough action. Edmund felt the nerves in the whole ship vibrating with it. And then it was up the lift, like an offering, bursting through mechanical guts into the world, and more waiting.

His own guts were already like hot soup. And there was little to do but sit, the Sutton harness chafing at his shoulders, the Sun turning the cockpit into a concentrated mass of hot air and hotter surfaces despite the canopy being wound fully back. The fact that they were sailing downwind until the call to launch didn't help. There was only so many times he could trudge through the pre-flight procedures. Check controls, trim settings, everything ready to start the engine. Gunsight? Brightness full. Wingspan to sixty-five feet, right for a Junkers Eighty-Eight and a Savoia

Marchetti, though he could change it quickly enough. He occupied himself looking at the radar aerial swinging to and fro to see if Tricky up in the control room was picking anything up, and gazing, unfocussed at the other ships in Force X. The battleship *Malaya* was level with *Eagle* and thumping impressively through the swell. Still, couldn't let the attention wander too far. Had to keep an eye on Wings up in the bridge every so often in case he was signalling for them to start up.

Eventually, the signal came. There were no reports of raids, it was just to relieve the duty patrol. He primed the engine, hit the starter, the Merlin whine-cough-crashed into a lumpy growl and the mechanics disconnected the accumulator trolley. Edmund's hands almost developed will of their own. It took physical effort to stop them starting the take-off until everyone was clear. Check oil pressure, temp, boost... Finally, he was free to open the throttle and felt the Hurricane start to strain against the brakes. A final check that the prop was in fine, and he let the tail come up in the slipstream, balancing for a moment on the mainwheels alone - the view opening up over the deck to the bow and then the sparking sea - before letting the brakes off and feeling the aircraft lunge forward.

Eagle had a good bit of breeze over the deck and Edmund felt the wheels leave before he was even halfway along. He pushed the nose down a touch to let the speed build, retracted gear and flaps, and set the prop pitch for the climb. He closed the canopy and for a moment the cockpit was greenhouse-oppressive, reeking of oil, hot metal, old leather. Edmund secured his oxygen mask, the weeping rubber momentarily disgusting until he surrendered to the discomfort and accepted it.

The Hurricane was perfectly horrible until the trim had been adjusted. He'd barely got it as close to hands and feet off as Hurri One ever did and settled into best climbing speed, before Tricky's voice crackled onto the strangled radio. "Yellow section, steer zero-nine-zero, make angels ten, over."

He acknowledged and steered east as directed. When they reached about ten miles in front of the convoy, they'd begin to orbit. No point in asking Tricky if there was any trade, he'd tell them quickly enough if there was.

Once up, there was little to look at but the fuel gauge. He kept a good look out for aircraft anyway, but it was hard to pay as much attention knowing that of all the radars down there in the escort, none had picked anything up. He adjusted the throttle and leaned out the mixture as much as possible, to spin out the patrol. If they were lucky they would be able to get about an hour and a quarter in the air, which would diminish considerably if there were any chasing or fighting to do. The R/T remained stubbornly silent. No contacts. The convoy pressed on beneath, miniature ships inching along a sheet of mercury. Two and a half days from Malta. How many would make it? Would any?

Two and a half days. And they were already in range of enemy aircraft. And that was without the subs that would be out here. And what had Vickery said? There were Italian cruisers out!

The fuel gauge ticked down. No contacts. The orbit stretched out endlessly. When the needle touched fifteen gallons, he radioed the ship and was ordered to return. Tricky vectored them on to *Eagle* and they began to let down. The next patrol would be launching about now.

Five minutes later, the R/T hissed and Tricky came on the air. "Shadower. Junkers Eighty-Eight. Visual contact from *Eagle*, five miles distant, working round south, approx angels three. Blue section, vector two-three-zero, buster."

Blue leader acknowledged. Damn! Just as Yellow section was finishing the patrol. What rotten fortune.

"Yellow leader, report fuel state."

They might get to join in. Might just have enough juice.

Looked at the fuel gauge, tapped it. "Ten gallons. How much fuel Yellow Two?" he asked.

"Eleven gallons," Yeates replied.

"Return to ship, Yellow Section" Tricky ordered.

Balls! Edmund huffed and followed the course they'd been given. *Eagle* was now hurrying in the opposite direction to the convoy. He scanned around for the snooper, but it would be on the other side of the ship, near enough ten miles away. Damn it. He listened to Tricky vectoring Blue onto the shadower, Blue One and Blue Two engaging, hitting it, damaging it, the stern chase that developed. It had a head start, and Blue having to climb hard to reach it didn't help. Oh, if only they'd detected it a bit earlier! Two minutes. One minute, just one.

Nothing to be done about it now. He passed the carrier downwind and turned back onto the approach. Hook down, flaps down, wheels down, canopy back. Every time from the first that he had landed on a carrier - *Eagle* in particular - Edmund experienced the same bubble of almost-panic as he began the curving, descending run that led to the flight deck. *You expect me to land on that?* The tiny speck of flat grey in the middle of the wrinkled ocean, even dwarfed by the stripe of its own white wake. *Eagle* was worse than most because she was an old carrier, and small, and her flight deck narrowed at the stern and tapered away completely at the bow, unlike the wide rectangle of the newer ships. She seemed stationary at this distance, the funnel smoke like something cast in clay. If you fixed on that, eventually you would notice it changing, gradually like peacetime clouds tumbling on a summer's day. The movement of the ship would accelerate as you closed, first a forward snail-motion apparent, then the somnolent rise and fall of the deck. And then finally, as the distance vanished, the thundering, roaring, blasting through the sea at twenty-five knots. The pyroclastic torrent of funnel smoke and turbulence whipping the Hurricane around while the insect DLCO down by the deck jabbed his bats - too high, too low, too port, too starboard - and you cajoled the controls to answer him, and then in an instant preparing for the impact or pushing the throttle to miss the ship and do it all over again. If it was the former a *krnth-whup*! through the whole airframe and a heave on the shoulders as the hook caught or the ghastly nothing of missing everything and sailing on to dive over the bow or narrow-escape into the sky again.

This time the Hurricane made it down, the hook bit the wire, and he felt a momentary assault of shock and relief that somehow the inevitable disaster had not come to fruition. He was then throttling the engine down, releasing the wheel brakes to let the maintainers unhook the wire and roll the Hurri back to the lift. Brakes back on and already the ship was rising around him to swallow the Hurricane with him still inside it, until the machine was in the crowded hangar. He pulled the securing pin from the Sutton harness and peeled his sweat-soaked body out of the aircraft. Was it only just over an hour since he'd taken off?

"Bad luck, sir," Mac said as he helped Edmund down, took his Mae West and the bundle of emergency gubbins. "Just a few minutes, I hear. You'll get one next time, mark my words."

Edmund grimaced, tried to show gratitude, and feeling worthless, fled. He changed into dry clothes and went up to the pilots' crew room for a bit, but it was rather crowded and the chatter hurt his ears. He tried the goofer's, where Crosley was attempting to film activity on deck with his cine camera, and grabbed a mug of tea and a corned beef sandwich from a rating lugging a tray of provisions around to the dutymen. Despite the early appearance of a shadower, the day had not turned out as he...indeed, as everyone seemed to have expected. Apart from the odd report of an aircraft buzzing around the perimeter of the convoy there had been nothing. No raids. Range was still a bit high, but not excessively so for the crates with the longest endurance. Perhaps the Eyetie fleet was coming out. Perhaps there'd be a surface battle, and all these fighters the carrier was loaded with would be next to useless. He sighed, tried to force down the last of the sandwich, which lay like a pound of wet cement in his stomach.

It would be a couple more hours until he was needed to fly again, assuming the Regia Aeronautica and Luftwaffe didn't decide to descend on them *en masse* this afternoon. It wasn't beyond the realms of possibility, nor did it strike Edmund as especially likely. Bastards were saving it all up for the morrow. After all, it didn't matter to them when they hit the convoy, as long as it failed to reach Malta.

Activity had calmed somewhat, and the anticipation of action had waned. All at once, it was just as it had been first thing this morning, with only Edmund and Vickery standing at the rail. They acknowledged each other once again with a nod - and said nothing. Vickery started jotting a few lines in a small notebook, but the increasing headwind kept trying to flap the right-hand page over against his hand. He slipped book and pencil into a pocket and took a long breath, in and out. "Le vent se lève!" he said.

"...*Il faut tenter de vivre*!" Edmund continued automatically. "*L'air immense ouvre et referme mon livre*. You know Paul Valéry."

"Not well," Vickery replied. "I met him once or twice in the late twenties."

"Oh, I meant..."

Vickery grinned. "A feature of getting old. To the young, you seem to come out of history. While for you it's just memory."

"I didn't tell you about my third and fourth kill, did I?" blurted Edmund. Why on Earth had he said that? Something about the mention of getting old, when he thought of the unlikelihood of that fate being his...

Vickery's smile became kinder. "No, but please don't feel you have to justify yourself to me. I can get the reports. The ones the Admiralty see fit to share, anyway."

Edmund shook his head. "You won't get a damned thing from those. No, I haven't had time to tell you much about the third, although that's the one I regret most, in a way. I should go on to the fourth - that's the real corker - but that would be wrong." He was babbling now. What were these words that were coming out of his mouth?

"Regret?" Vickery raised an eyebrow.

Edmund pursed his lips. "Wish I could explain. The fourth. That's the one that really shows how things are." How *fraudulent* all this was. How corrupt. "But first things first. The third. It was a temporary posting to the RN Fighter Flight in Egypt. There weren't enough carriers for all the pilots at that point, so we were helping out the RAF in the Western Desert."

Third kill
23 January 1942

Combat report Sub Lieutenant E.G. Clydesdale RNVR, RN Fighter Squadron Dekheila. Hurricane IIB 'G'

"Convoy protection patrol along coast. Approx 70 miles N of Fuka encountered formation of 6 Ju88 about to carry out a shallow dive-bombing attack on a coastal convoy. Engaged lead A/C immediately and all E/A jettisoned bombs and attempted to escape into cloud. Pursued one E/A, engaging whenever it emerged from cloud, making stern and quarter attacks. Made one attack, scoring hits, just as E/A entered cloud and some moments later observed it falling out of control, apparently having broken into two large sections, which fell into the sea near an escorting destroyer. At this point realised that wingman, Mids. A.J. Leonard, had become separated, and could not raise him on R/T. Searched, but returned to Dekheila when fuel ran low."

***

Two Hurricanes hung in the depthless blue pool. Below, a skein of white puffs, and beneath that, if you looked hard, a darker blue that was the sea, and off to the left a fawn tinge through the haze that was the land. If you didn't look closely, the Hurricanes might be suspended in limitless space.

Edmund was looking closely. Were those 'grazing sheep' clouds getting thicker, closer together? He stared, as if trying to bore through the cloud and haze with the energy he was pouring into his gaze.

Ah, there it was. A streak of white in black, and another, and another, through a channel between clouds. The convoy, still on course, and roughly on time. "What do you make our position, Leonard?" he asked his wingman.

The pause was longer than he liked but after a moment, Leonard's voice crackled through his earphones. "Fuka at one-six-zero, seventy miles."

"Alright. Your fuel?"

"About seventy-five gallons."

"Alright. I've got about seventy-eight."

Silence descended again. Edmund began a search of the sky in the forward hemisphere again. He and Leonard were at eight thousand feet. They could expect that any bombers would arrive at about the same altitude, or a bit higher. When they first began these convoy patrols, the Junkers' tended to come in at no more than five or six thousand, but since the Navy's Fulmars and Hurricanes started making more interceptions, they were getting higher. Eight or ten. That was good. However frustrating, it meant that they were having an effect. And every thousand feet the Jerries added to their height meant a greater chance their bombing would be inaccurate.

Edmund resisted the temptation to carry on his search behind, to glance in the mirror. That was what Leonard was there for. The backs of his hands started to prickle. Ever since that ME had almost got him, the idea of leaving the sky behind to someone else to worry about... He searched ahead again, dividing the sky up, scanning each section, riven with the knowledge there could be a fleet of machines out there that his eyes could just be skating over.

Ahead, the gentle undulations of the cloud were growing into towers and stacks. On the horizon, a city of cloud. In a couple of minutes, the city had drawn near, its towers and turrets budding and accreting as he watched. The patches below were converging into a carpet. Annoying. He flew the two of them into the city, skirting vast minarets of cloud, catching sight of his aircraft's shadow, ringed with a bright corona, skimming along the surface before the shadow of another tower fell across it.

And there, against a pinnacle to his right. Even as he checked again, the lurch in his chest told him it was so. Somehow, in the heat, every part of him already slicked with sweat, he noticed his palms perspiring even more. A cluster of specks a little higher, flying parallel to them. A formation of aircraft.

"Three o'clock, level," he said. "Bandits."

"I see them." Leonard replied so quickly Edmund wondered if he'd already sighted the enemy machines but didn't like to say so. He'd have to deal with that when they got back.

"Alright, stay on me. They don't seem to see us yet. I'm going to work around into a quartering position. We can use the cloud. If we get separated, whatever you do don't make a stern attack. Make sure you keep an eye on your fuel and head back before you get down to twenty gallons."

"OK, Flight Leader."

"Tally ho," he said, feeling the thrill of the words thrum through him over the anxiety, and banked his Hurricane smartly to starboard. The two Hurricanes skirted around the top of a tumbled ziggurat of cumulus, and for a moment were out in clear sky again. Edmund started to climb to build up overtaking speed and kept his focus on the bombers - as they surely were, now, the twin engine nacelles were visible bulges beneath the strip of the fuselage. Six of them, in a loose formation. Edmund had already fixed his mind on the lead aeroplane. It would be easier to shoot one down if he picked off the tail-end Charlie, but the point was to disrupt the bombing attack. Another kill would be nice...show the bastards in the wardroom who looked down their aquiline noses at him...but a well-intercepted raid, a convoy protected would do that just as well.

It wasn't a bad interception. The bombers - Junkers Eighty-Eights - entered a shallow dive to start their run in on the convoy, and only saw the two Hurricanes when they were five hundred yards away. Edmund had begun to dive too, to gather a bit of speed with the aim of pulling up and attacking from below, and the IAS was ticking over 300 when the first tracers lashed out at him. The bombers swelled in the canopy, black and solid, and then he pulled the nose up, hitting the gun button when the reflector sight swam onto the target. The gunfire played on the Junkers for half a second, and then the top side of the machine was facing him, paint flashing in the sun, and the formation shattered as each aircraft turned away. He caught a glimpse of a sort of black snow -strings of jettisoned bombs tumbling into space. They'd already done it. The convoy was safe. But Edmund stuck to the lead aircraft, the Junkers was there, contorting and knotting in the gunsight. Disengaging now made no sense. He glanced around. No other aircraft.

"Where are the others, Leonard?" he puffed, hard manoeuvring making the words difficult to get out.

"All gone. Heading north in ones and twos."

Edmund got in another good burst at the leader, ignoring his own advice not to make a stern attack - with the G that the Junkers was pulling the gunner wouldn't be able to get a good bead on him for a few seconds. It reversed its turn. Another decent short burst, flashes flickered around the fuselage, and the bomber put its nose down, framed beautifully against a mass of white cloud. Edmund lined the sight up again... Then, balls to it. The Ju88 had disappeared into the marble flank. He made a quick calculation of where the aircraft would emerge - it would have to stay straight and level, trying to manoeuvre in that clag could be suicide even with functioning instruments - and turned the Hurricane closer, aiming to skirt around the edge. Whether he misjudged or the cloud was blowing, collapsing, faster in the wind than he had allowed for, he clipped the edge of it. A momentary surprise as the world disappeared, visibility of miles instantly shortened to a few feet. The aircraft bumped as though there were thicker lumps in the white mass, and then he was through. Edmund levelled out. The plane was now swimming above a carpet of soft whiteness, unbroken through to the world below. Where's the Junkers? Aha, got you! The bomber puffed out of the cloud face roughly where he thought it would, and immediately turned to starboard, fleeing for the next bit of cover. It had gained on him in the cloud but now had to turn across his bows. Edmund pushed the throttle through the gate, overboosting the engine for a moment, and the prop bit harder in the air as the Hurricane raced downhill. The Eighty-Eight had set itself up for a quarter attack, and he turned with it, blasting out with his twelve machine guns - why, oh, why didn't they have cannon yet! - but then the Junkers disappeared again.

He was in a forest of cloud needles thrusting up from the main mass below. Edmund's aeroplane darted between them, following a glimpse here, another there. "Leonard, are you with me?" he called, remembering far too late in the engagement to check on his wingman. The response was garbled, the radio signal sounding broken. Damn it. But there was the Junkers again. He got in another good burst with the last of his ammunition just as the bomber entered the top of a cloud stack, and thought he saw pieces flying off the tail. He'd left it too late to avoid. In a moment he was in the cloud too, encased in grey, rain splattering against the canopy. Edmund throttled back, keeping straight and level, heart juddering in his ribcage, staring at the grey nothing ahead, praying the sharp cross of a Junkers didn't lunge out of it. He throttled back more. Bloody hell. "Leonard, are you on me?" he radioed again. A metallic shriek cut through the radio then abruptly stopped. He was not going to emerge from the cloud like this. "I'm descending to clear the cloud," he added, checking the mirror and glancing over his shoulder. He couldn't even see his own wingtip. There was no way Leonard could follow him in this clag. "Leonard, maintain course, three-three-zero, reduce speed and descend in steps," he called, and turned his own Hurricane thirty degrees to the west. It was too late really, but he should ensure there was some separation between them, assuming his wingman had followed him into the cloud. He had no way of knowing.

This time there was no reply at all. Bugger. His radio must be on the blink. Edmund kept his eyes glued to the artificial horizon, holding the wings level as though they were his arms and he were balancing on a beam above an abyss. In a moment the Hurricane thumped out of the murk. Thank Christ! Another scan to get his bearings...there was the convoy, white slashes on the sea a little back and to the left, and...above it, a spinning, tumbling form. He registered a second form just as the Junkers plunged noiselessly into the sea, barely missing a destroyer on the convoy's flank. The wreckage bobbed in plume of the warship's bow wave and disappeared. Well, at least there should be confirmation. The JU must have broken up as it fell. He'd definitely scored hits on the tail. Perhaps the rudder or elevator had been damaged. He flicked the radio switch and put out a call to Leonard. Nothing. Where the hell was his wingman? Edmund checked his fuel state and began to orbit, calling and calling again, answered only by static.

***

13 June 1942

Every inch of Edmund's skin went cold, and it had nothing to do with the breeze. A sudden unnatural chill. A haunting of air.

When he'd flown them into the cloud, like an idiot, like a novice, Edmund had throttled back and descended. What if Leonard hadn't? Had he just kept ploughing on into the cloud at full throttle, on the last course Edmund had steered them onto - directly after the Junkers? He'd told Leonard to slow down but by then it was probably far too late.

"It's all very uncertain," Vickery said, cautiously. "But you did hit the Junkers, and it did crash..."

"So did Leonard. Crash, that is. At least, he must've done. We don't actually know. Nobody does. We probably never will. All because I piled on into the cloud. And when I got back I was still more bothered about claiming the bloody kill than I was about Leonard!" His voice had begun to run away, too loud, and he shut it down.

"As far as you knew he might have landed elsewhere - or was

still on his way."

Had he? Had he thought that? "I don't know... I knew what the state of our fuel was. I was annoyed with him for getting lost! Can you imagine!" Edmund covered his face with his hands. "When I stopped searching for him, I thought he'd be on his way home. But even when I got there and he hadn't arrived or called in..."

"You don't know Leonard *didn't* get lost or disoriented and simply crash..."

"He wouldn't have been in the cloud if it hadn't been for me."

"You didn't fly into the cloud on purpose. And in combat, you have to make split-second decisions." Vickery smiled, tightly. "I carry such things myself, you know. I avoided getting myself into positions of responsibility just so I didn't have to worry about having men's lives on my conscience, which was cowardly even if I didn't regard myself as ready. But there are times I still wonder if I'd done this or that differently, one or two fellows might still be alive."

Edmund shrugged. It wasn't hypothetical. He'd as good as killed Leonard.

"I know I won't convince you," Vickery said, as though he'd anticipated Edmund's train of thought, "but try to put the worry aside until a better time. You'll want to examine all this one day, but now is not the time. Not when there are more immediate concerns."

Examine all this... Good heavens, that was the last thing he wanted.

Was that why he almost hoped it would end, this trip?

Vickery patted him on the arm. "You know. The fact that you're torn up about it means you're still human. That there's a fundamentally decent core. And I think that's what I came out here to see."

Edmund stared. It made no sense to him. With the killing, and the killing becoming a game. Where was the room for decency? He shook his head, as if shaking off the thoughts themselves, and made his excuses.

Yellow Section went up again later that day, but it was little different. A report of a single aircraft on the other side of the convoy that was gone by the time his section had launched and climbed to height. Another just after he had landed. The Germans and Italians were laughing at them. Taunting them, with what would come tomorrow, while they wore out their handful of Hurricanes chasing shadows and whispers. It was inevitable. Tomorrow there would have to be a reckoning.

DAY 2
14 June 1942

It was Sunday. It didn't feel like a Sunday. No Sunday service on the flight deck. Only Sea Hurricanes lined up and waiting for the signal. 'Wings' must have got over excited as Yellow was first off. Edmund was still rubbing the sleep out of his eyes as his engine was run up at just after Oh-Seven-Hundred. He barely felt awake as he opened the throttle to take off, late correcting the swing on the rudder and wandering all over the deck. Yeates, behind, must have wondered what in the blazes was going on although it was equally possible he was just as beaten up.

Three quarters of an hour of stooging around trying not to admire the view, the neat rows of ships mathematically scoring the cobalt sea, ears sore with alertness for the announcement of bogies. And once again, the call only came when Yellow Section was on the way down, low on fuel, Pink climbing into the still-lightening sky to intercept. They came back reporting damage to a Ju88. First blood, and it was a drop in the ocean. Then Red Flight flew off at 0920 and White half an hour later, just as a Savoia-Marchetti appeared. They flogged their Hurris mercilessly getting to it at twelve thousand feet - and managed to get a few hits before it out-distanced them.

Edmund waited his turn, numb, insides seething. Today there would not be long to wait. They'd be trying to keep as many Hurricanes in the air as possible once the raids started. Yellow was held back while the CO and Hutton went up again. There were six of them up now.

And yet, still nothing seemed to be happening.

"Bloody hell," someone said and a moment later a *thud-thu-thu-sssshhhh!-thu-thump-sssshhhh!* carried over the water to the flight deck. Edmund, standing by his Hurricane turned towards it, saw *Argus* seemingly sailing through a winter pine forest, the trees spearing up then collapsing into melted discs on the surface of the sea. The old carrier leaned to port, then to starboard, its wake warping and turning. And a tide of relief, she was OK. *Eagle*'s goofers' erupted in laughter and scattered applause.

Edmund looked up, into the sun, sneezed, held his thumb over the burning blob in the sky. Was there a wisp of contrail through the cirrus? Bombing from high altitude. That was good to know. But that stick had been accurate. A few feet this way or that and *Argus* would be on the bottom.

"They're going for the carriers first, then," he murmured when the excitement had died down, and at that everyone's nearby turned their faces skyward, one or two peering at the 279 aerial to see if the radar was tracking something. But surely *Malaya*, to the north, with her newer radar, would detect the incoming bogies sooner.

As if in response, a rating messenger emerged from the island and ran aft, to where the Hurricanes were being prepared for launch. "There's a large raid coming in," he puffed, "Get ready now, Wings'll tip you the wink as soon as you're buttoned up.

Fingers trembling, Edmund ran through the starting procedure, forcing himself to be precise, to not rush anything. That was the surest way to make sure the engine failed to start or threw something as soon as the taps were opened. When he was sure, he put his hand up, finger pointing skywards and motioning a circle, then hit the starter.

Once in the air, he had just about pulled everything up and closed the canopy when Tricky crackled over the R/T. "You're on your own Yellow One. Yellow Two went U/S on deck. Vector zero-nine-zero, climb 'buster', angels eight. Lots of bogies on this track, about twenty miles. Good hunting."

Very well, alone.

The solitary Hurricane climbed at full power, propeller yanking at the air to haul it to eight thousand feet. Edmund dashed off some calculations, a bit of trigonometry and worked out he'd be at the appointed area in about six minutes. Six minutes of engine softly roaring, a few faint voices cutting through the R/T now and again, some that might have been Italian. His heart seemed to be lurching out of his chest and trying to grapple with his Sutton harness.

When the last seconds ticked down he was about to ask Tricky for more instructions, when he saw them. He gaped under his oxygen mask. Easiest spot he'd ever made. Coming in from the east, a thousand feet above him. A beautiful balbo of SM Seventy-Nines, bellies creamy-grey in the morning sun and all lined up just for him. Tricky had placed him up sun - thank you Tricky! - and if he'd only had another thousand feet... He pulled the tit for the boost override and felt the Hurri buck forward. They were crossing a little from right to left, and he wouldn't have much overtaking speed. Come on engine, just keep pulling... They were still behind, he still had time...almost at the same level now, and space to turn on the beam...can't line up the first one or the second...will have to be arse-end Charlie.

The Savoia bumbled into the gunsight, across the deflection ring, and Edmund hit the trigger. Tracers looped out...he pressed on in until the Hurri was bouncing in the slipstream and then hauled away, diving to pick up speed and pulling up again. Just then, he heard a hiss on the radio and "Tally ho!" in his ears. It was Red and Black sections, already in the air and attacking together. Edmund watched them diving in, one at a time, peppering the bombers and curving away. The formation shattered, a slow-motion bomb-burst, and flurries of black rain briefly fell from each. *Bastards can't do any damage now*, he thought, but it was forced. *Why couldn't they have given me a few more minutes alone?* Now all the claims would be shared. He picked a Savoia that was best placed for him to have a go at and got another burst out at it.

But then Tricky was on the R/T, calling "more bogies, lots of the bastards, bearing two-two-zero, angels ten. Ten miles." Edmund cursed to himself and tagged on to the formation. The five Hurricanes hurried to the scene. There were indeed lots of the bastards. Edmund only had a couple of seconds of ammunition left...*spend it wisely... don't open fire too far out, stay precise, don't 'hose' the target...* They didn't fully break that raid up. There were too many formations. Edmund caught a glimpse of patterns of white flowers erupting around the ships below and prayed none of the bombs hit.

And then back to *Eagle*. The Hurricanes descended and curved around onto a path that would take them to the deck. Edmund found his eyes drawn to clusters of black spots. He was about to call 'break' when the spots faded, another set appeared. Balls. Ack-ack. Just then a crash resounded through the airframe, followed a second later by a sound like rain on the fuselage behind him. Bloody hell, they were shooting at him. "Tricky, can't you get the fishheads to lay off shooting at us?" he snapped into the R/T as he tried to make the Hurricane weave.

"Trying old chap, they're not very trusting," the controller answered. The ack-ack did not abate, and Edmund found himself dodging between the thickest patches of it. Mercifully, *Eagle* was away from the main body of ships, steaming hard in the opposite direction. After a few minutes running the gauntlet, he passed out of the worst of it.

It was only when they'd landed that Edmund realised there were only four Hurricanes. He read across the code letters. It was Red Two who was missing. The CO's wingman. When he extracted himself from the cockpit, he asked Spike what happened. The pilot shrugged. "Hutton bought it. Tried to stern-chase a JU Eighty-Eight. Last I saw of him he was diving away on fire."

"Christ," Edmund breathed. "Hope he got out." Hutton. Hutton didn't like him. That didn't seem to matter.

"Didn't look like it," Spike replied, and turned for the washroom.

Bizarrely, for the first time that day, the spasms of activity on deck had calmed. It seemed that the Italians had stopped for lunch. After the big raid Edmund had recently been in action against, there had been no more bogies on the fleet's radar screens. The RDF operators and controllers were waiting at their stations, wondering at the blankness of it all. They'd be back alright. But for now, there was breathing space. The deck crew walked to the Hurricanes instead of running, chatted to each other as they pushed the machine back to the lift.

In the hangar, if anything, the frenzy was worse than before. Edmund watched as unserviceable aircraft were pushed to the corners, struck down, spare aircraft brought forward. The hangar deck was littered with cowling panels, and half a dozen Hurricanes had developed infestations of clambering mechanics. Edmund changed into dry clothes and sauntered to the goofer's. He had an hour or so. Time to grab a bite to eat, half a cup of tea, perhaps exchange a word or two with Vickery.

Why was that important? With a hollow swoop he realised it was because he'd like the old reporter to be the last person he spoke to. Properly spoke to.

Of course the mess fires were all out, the stoves' oil drained away to prevent flash fires, but the galley party were threading their way through the ship handing out mess traps with cold meat and pickles out of a tin, mugs of soup that the cook had managed to heat through with the galley's steam supply. At the smell of the soup Edmund felt a sudden hunger, and managed to more or less fill his growling belly before pre-combat nausea began to assert itself again. He had only begun to wonder where he might find Vickery before it was time to head back to the hangar, when the journalist appeared bearing a jingling stack of empty mess tins. "Oh hello," he said, peering round the enamelware tower. "I was just making myself useful."

"Here, I'll give you a hand." Edmund lifted part of the pile of tins gingerly off the top, added his own and fell into step with Vickery as they headed back to the galley.

"So," Edmund said when they'd dropped off the tableware. "Are you getting lots of material?"

"Enough for a book or two, never mind the papers," Vickery sighed. "I'll have to write something properly substantial when...when I get the time."

Edmund smiled grimly to himself. No-one wanted to tempt fate by talking about when the war might be over these days. Many of them wouldn't see it. And just being over did not necessarily mean their troubles might be ended, but just beginning. The way Rommel was driving back the army in Egypt...well, that might close off the Eastern Med, and then the Suez Canal might be lost, and that would probably be the end of the whole theatre. Then Hitler could devote his attentions properly to the Soviets, and after that, Britain again...

Whichever way they cut it, for Malta to hang on was vital. "When do you suppose that might be?"

"I was thinking of retiring next year." Vickery tried to smile but there was no humour in his eyes. "I'm not getting any younger. Time to hand over to someone with a bit more vitality."

"Let's make sure you have a convoy to remember, then." Edmund regretted the words as soon as they were out of his mouth, but Vickery just laughed.

"Oh, I don't doubt it will be, one way or another."

"How is the convoy doing?" Edmund asked, feeling as though it was belated. "All the ships alright?"

Vickery looked away for a moment. "A pack of torpedo bombers got past the low escort. They got one of the merchantmen. Er, *Tanimbar*, I think. And a cruiser. HMS *Liverpool*? She's still afloat, or was the last thing I heard, but in a pretty bad way and limping back to Gib."

"Christ. Really?" Edmund rubbed his brow. "That spreads us a bit thin for AA cover."

Viciously, Edmund thought *at least there'll be a bit less of it firing at me*, and regretted that too. Losing *Liverpool* halved the convoy's cruiser cover.

They stood for a moment, looking at each other awkwardly. Edmund glanced at his watch. "Well if you aren't too busy," he said, "there's the matter of my fourth and so-far final kill to clear up."

"Oh?" Vickery was keeping his expression neutral, but Edmund thought he saw flashes of curiosity and concern warring there.

"It's self-indulgent, I know. It's just..." Edmund looked at the deck. "I know you were sent here to write about me. I shall end up in one of those HMSO paperbacks, shan't I?"

Vickery nodded gently. "I dare say. Something like that."

"I don't suppose it'll make any difference to the way they write it. But just for one person out there to know how it really was. Does that make sense?"

Vickery drew himself up, just a touch, transforming as he did so into a kind of priest. "Yes. Yes it does."

"All right then. My fourth kill. Just last month. Operation 'Ironclad', you'll remember - the landings on Madagascar."

Fourth kill
7 May 1942

Maybe this was the day they'd finally meet the Vichy French air force. There'd been precious little sight of them thus far. The word was they had a dozen modern Potez twin-engined fighters, something a bit like a Bf110, and a similar number of single-seaters out here on Madagascar. Dewoitines or Morane-Saulniers. You wouldn't have known it. Other than the odd reconnaissance kite, dashing in at high speed to see what the commandos were doing and dashing away again before the controllers had a chance to vector a patrol. Edmund couldn't hide his disappointment. Facing the Luftwaffe was one thing. He still felt his guts turn to water when there was a real chance of that...but the French, with their inferior aircraft and stuck out here where they were surely out of practice...it was supposed to be a cakewalk. A rare chance at a fairground coconut shy. The squadron pilots had talked each other into ludicrous bets as to who would get the most kills, and whether anyone would make 'ace in a day'. No-one had bet on him, of course. Though he'd already got three kills, as many as anyone in the squadron, nobody quite believed it. His gunnery scores in training, his flying reports - consistently rated 'average' - didn't square with it. He'd heard one rumour that he'd been Bader's wingman in the Battle of Britain and that Bader had gifted him a kill. And the others had just been luck, of course.

Luck.

Edmund glanced to port and starboard to check the members of his flight were all in position, wingman to starboard and the second section off to port and a little behind. First time leading a flight and he didn't want to mess it up. The itching temptation to thumb the mic button and say something like *close up Blue Two!*... But he resisted. Honestly, he was happier with the formation loose. Easier to keep clear of one another, and greater freedom to keep an eye out for bogies. He felt a little guilty over it. Poor technique. Better that than another...than a collision.

Beneath, the sea was luminous blue-green, an impossible colour, ahead a buff slash that was the coast. He started the flight climbing gently until they had fifteen hundred feet on the clock, then nosed downward a touch, the ASI winding up so they crossed the coast at two hundred and seventy-five. There were pongoes down there, dug in, and they'd shoot at anything that flew, so better to be going like the devil when they passed. There were the scars of fortification down there, and beyond, columns of troops moving forward. There'd be more further ahead, the advance guard, and then the scouting parties.

Once they'd passed the rear echelon of troops, he resisted to urge to check with the flight that they'd avoided any damage. He hadn't noticed gunfire, but you wouldn't with small arms unless something hit you. And not always then. He scanned over oil pressure, engine temps...all fine. If the others had any sense they'd be doing the same. No, radio silence until it was strictly necessary to break it. Bloody hell, his heart was going nineteen to the dozen. Calm it down, Clydesdale, calm it down. The urge to do something, anything, active, rather than just keep flying on. Searching the sky. Flying on.

A streak across the landscape, now passing below was the

road from Ambarata to Diego Suarez. In a moment they'd be in enemy territory proper. Now it was really time to keep a good search out. This was where they'd find the enemy, if he was coming up today.

There! A speck moving across the landscape. He'd seen a flash of sun off it, but damn it, he'd seen it first! "Bogey, two o'clock low," he said quickly, before someone else got in.

"I see them, flight leader," Haines replied. Them? "Three. MS Four-Oh-Sixes I think."

"Alright," Edmund replied, brushing off the annoyance that his wingman had pinned the number and type when he'd only seen one, and could not have told it from a lesser spotted shitehawk at this range. "Tally ho!"

He banked to starboard, tracking the flecks - yes, there did seem to be three of them - across the low hill. Definitely a smudge of red and yellow, the ID markings the Vichy kites wore, on the leader.

And then, "Break!" jabbed in his ears. Ellis. He had no time to curse his rotten luck as he hauled the Hurricane to port, the flight 'scissoring' into two pairs at the pre-arranged signal. Why, curse it? There must have been more of the bastards.

"Where are they Ellis?" he cried, huffing against the G as the fighter curved around.

"Climbing up for another attack," Ellis responded. "Four of them. Yo-yo-ing, reverse your turn."

Edmund rolled the Hurricane to port, the ground lurching over above him for a second as he passed through the inverted. He used the momentum to pull the aircraft back into another steep banking turn to the right. The Moranes must be over to the left somewhere now, higher.

As if in response to his thought, Haines hissed "four o'clock, high, Blue leader."

"Got them!" Edmund reversed the turn again, climbing hard,

just as the Moranes did the same, and in a second the two gaggles were heading at each other on a collision course. Edmund just had time to line one up, press the gun button when they'd broken away again. He pulled round in pursuit, remembered there were two other knots of French fighters around, reversed the turn again. The French couldn't get at them like this. Not if they just kept turning hard. With the Moranes doing the same, a couple of times more Edmund found himself head-on to a pair of the fighters, lined up, fired - even scored a few hits, at least there were flashes and puffs of smoke on the target - and then they were gone, pulling Gs and puffing to breathe as grey pressed in around the edges of his vision.

"They're making a run for it," someone said in his ears, so distorted he couldn't even tell who. "Heading South, low level."

"OK, return to the carrier. Check fuel and for damage." Just then, in his peripheral vision, a heliotrope flare. When his brain caught up - explosion, on a hillside. A greasy thrust of smoke. Jesus!

"Blue flight, report!" he yelled.

"Blue two here."

"Blue three here."

"Blue four, here."

Bloody hell. The relief was like a cold bath. And then a second later, a surge of something else, ugly, invigorating. They'd got one. They'd shot one of the bastards down.

***

14 June 1942

Edmund opened the door and poked his head inside the wardroom. "Won't be a sec," he said to the surgeon, who grunted in response, then motioned Vickery inside.

"Now. I want to show you something." Edmund led Vickery

to a cabinet in a corner of the room. He unlocked it, removed a large book, something like a cross between a photo album and a church bible, and laid it down on the top. Gold lettering, already scuffed and word, on the cover read '801 Naval Air Squadron Line Book'. "Did you have these in the last war?"

"Oh yes," Vickery said. His eyes were saucers. He knew the significance of such a thing. The whole life of the squadron was to be found in here. Far more than the dry pages of the operations record book that would constitute the 'official' history. Edmund stepped back and gestured to Vickery to help himself. The journalist flicked through, pausing over cartoons drawn directly onto the pages, newspaper clippings and signals from Admirals praising the squadron's work, photos, poems, jokes... Onto these pages were poured the characters of men who in many cases would have no more life beyond what was distilled onto these papers. And something indefinable, and as fragile as it was indestructible - the character of the squadron.

"This page first." Edmund leafed to the last third of the book and smoothed out a page pasted with news clippings.

"It's all about you," Vickery breathed.

"Hmm," Edmund answered. "Yes. And no. Read this one."

He pointed. In amongst the more conventional headlines on small pieces was a larger, banner headline - CLYDESDALE'S FROG, it proclaimed. Above the text was a garish illustration of a Hurricane on the tail of another fighter, on fire and one wing snapping off. Edmund had never fully read the article. A lurid tale from a regional paper, declaring ownership of him - he'd been born in that part of England, though he hadn't lived there since the age of three - and his destruction of the Morane-Saulnier MS.406, apparently single-handed. "Frenchie makes four!" a sub-header added, pointing out that Clydesdale only needed one more kill and he'd be the Navy's first ace since Crete.

"And now this." He flicked over the page. Taking up the whole leaf was a beautifully rendered pen-and-ink illustration of a scroll, with a proclamation on it in elaborate Teutonic script:

'Hear Ye: Know all men by these letters that the officers herein mentioned did also sight and smite that Morane known henceforth as "Clydesdale's Frog": S/Lt Davis, Mid Ellis, Mid Haines'

"Oh." Vickery frowned. "So you all got a share?"

"Yes. No. I mean, we all hit at least one Morane. And one of them went in."

"But none of the others were mentioned in the coverage? That seems odd."

Edmund grimaced. "Not really. It's just easier if you read the combat report. Not my AC30, the squadron diary."

"I'd be allowed to see that? Without Ashley's say so?"

"I don't see why not. As long as you don't quote from it. Anyway, who's to know? This is just so you understand."

And it was. He wanted more than anything to be understood by this man, even as he fought against it. He reached into the cabinet and pulled out a second book.

"S/Lts Clydesdale and Davis and Mids Haines and Ellis started the ball rolling this morning by flying the first armed recce of the patrol. By 0630 they had crossed the Ambarata and Fort Bellvue-Antsirane road. By 0700 they had flown as far south as Mahagaga, a small village about 13 miles south of Antsirane. As they travelled down the line checking the state of enemy forward troops as they went, they observed three single engine bogies to the North West. The bogies were identified as MS406s, by which time the flight had assumed fighter battle formation and Mid Ellis noticed strings of red tracer streaming past sides of his fuselage. He cried 'break' over the R/T and the flight commenced a 'scissors'. It was soon apparent that four more Moranes waiting above were after each section of two Hurris but by continuing their break turns our aircraft presented practically impossible targets to the enemy who made no attempt to bracket.

"On one occasion a Morane came head-on to S/Lt Clydesdale and Mid Haines - they both fired - it broke away and proceeded to go head-on to S/Lt Davis and Mid Ellis - they both fired and registered hits. On another occasion a Morane pulled up in front of Ellis with its flaps out and he was surprised to find the range closing. He gave a long burst and noticed hits on the enemy's wings. This aircraft proceeded northwards at a reduced speed with two other Moranes in company. Meanwhile, the flight, still in its battle formation, managed a dozen or so more firing passes at Moranes head-on. The dog-fight lasted 4-5 minutes and then the Moranes disappeared as quickly as they had arrived - as they departed an aircraft was seen to crash into a hillside and blow-up. At first S/Lt Clydesdale believed this to be one of his flight and ordered a tell-off. However, when no4 came up 'loud and clear' it was realised that the Royal Navy had shot down its first Vichy fighter since Oran. S/Lt Clydesdale, as flight leader, is being credited with its destruction officially but the rest of the flight are claiming their one-quarter as well!"

Vickery cleared his throat awkwardly. "Is that customary? The flight leader is awarded any shared kills?"

"No. Never heard of it before or since. We were only told about a week after. The press notices had all gone out just with my name on. Heard back that only my claim had been verified, and it was for a whole kill."

The way they'd looked at him. Haines had barely said a word to him since.

"Well. I suppose you may as well have struck the fatal blow as anyone..."

"Balls," Edmund huffed. "We should have been awarded a

quarter each. Or if anything, Ellis should have been given it. He was probably the one who got it."

"It's...not a little unlike your first kill, no?" Vickery said gently.

"Not really. He didn't get bounced because he froze up, for one thing. Let's face it. The only reason was because I already had three. And I barely deserved those."

Vickery scratched his head, pulled a face. "I see how...uncomfortable this all is."

"Look. You can't write about it." Edmund rubbed his temples. A warm throb had just begun to pulse there. Headache coming on. Wonderful. He took a breath. "Don't you see, we can't have more of this! Why don't you write about the other chaps? The Skipper. He's held us together. Lewis-Evans. He's a bloody marvellous pilot, he has a knack for getting us all trained and prepared. And he knows why we're out here. You heard him. And the rest of them. All the pilots. The mechanics and maintainers, for that matter - they have to sit here under the bombs with nothing to wield but a spanner. Why can't you do a splash on them?"

"I will, of course. I intend to. But still. If you become an ace today or tomorrow, I can't very well not mention it. And if I manage to avoid it, the Navy will put out its own press notices anyway."

"Bugger. Yes, that's true. But you'll try to tell it as it is? Not like...like...," he turned the page and gestured at CLYDESDALE'S FROG.

"My boy." Vickery looked at him sidelong. "You can be utterly certain that nothing of that nature will come from my pen. Now, or ever."

Edmund laughed, despite himself. He felt lighter. "So, you understand?" Let them write their reports of his fifth kill, how he became an ace, and then that would be enough. Just one more. And then he could get on with the job without all this.

Vickery smiled and patted him lightly on the upper arm. "Yes, I think so. And I think one day, you will too."

What on Earth did that mean? Edmund frowned. "What is it you think I don't, exactly?" he said, trying to keep the irritation out of his voice.

"Perhaps I don't mean *understanding* as such. Perspective, then. You're doing the right thing, that's all I'll say."

"Right. Well." Edmund's sigh sent a little more of his courage, fortitude, whatever it was, leaking out of him. "Back to the fray."

One more. Just one more and they'd leave him alone. Of course. It was obvious. One more and his courage would return. One more and life would be simple again.

"Oh, Lieutenant?" the journalist said after Edmund had taken a few steps. "*Le vent se lève. Il faut tenter de vivre.*"

Edmund nodded, and made for his aircraft.

The wind rises. We must try to live.

Doesn't everyone deserve that, for a while at least?

The engine was already warm so just a couple of pumps on the ki-gas was enough to prime it, and it crashed into life as soon as he hit the starter. Checks, checks, checks... Magnetos OK for mag drop...gear and flap lever in the right place...tighten up the throttle friction...lock the canopy a couple of inches short of fully back - he'd let it go to the stop the first time he'd flown a Hurri and then couldn't get his fingers behind it to close when he was up, not until his fingernails had been shredded by the frame and his self-respect by his instructor...

And then up. The raids were coming thickly now, the R/T almost impenetrable with chatter. Lines of Junkers in echelon, Savoias in line astern coming across from Sicily. Lines and lines of them, stitching the sky. Tendrils of tracer licking out, debasing the cracked-glass sky. Edmund picked a formation and turned into the web. His Hurricane flung out streams of its own, hurtling into the stampede, bucking in the torn air of slipstreams, darting amongst weaving trimotors. The formation burst apart. For lambent moments the sky was deranged with aircraft. His engine was devouring petrol. His guns were vomiting ammunition. There was no time to concentrate on any one aircraft. After the first formation disintegrated, some Savoias ditching their bombs, Edmund looped up with Yellow Two and found the next, building up a good overtaking speed and blasting through it from above. As the fuel, ammunition, time ran down, they were wolves among reindeer. Savage. Blood-blind.

The bombers dispersed, diffused. They were still around, but their organisation was gone. Most were heading away. Edmund's fuel was low, ammunition almost gone. He had shot at half a dozen aircraft - and was certain he had scored hits on a few. But had he brought any down? No. Impossible to say. But no. He knew it. As the madness calmed, the need slammed down again. The questions would greet him as soon as he got back. Did you get one? Or, how many did you get? He scanned around. Any stragglers? A limping machine, easy meat?

The fuel gauge was screaming at him. Always allow a gallon for every minute of flight. It would take ten minutes to recover aboard, and he had eleven gallons. That would be OK if he could go straight in, but any hanging around, for a crash on deck, or to turn into wind...no, it was tighter than it should be anyway. His hands and feet, stiff with regret and frustration, guided the Hurricane towards *Eagle*'s beacon. There would be other chances today.

The patrol structure was on the brink of collapsing. As soon as a Hurricane hit the deck, it, and its pilot, were prepared to go back up again. Virtually every other pilot who'd flown against that last raid was claiming something. Two kills, two probables, and a handful of damaged. He almost decided not to even bother reporting the couple of machines he'd hit. The nakedness of it shocked him into cowardice, and he mentioned them like an insincere apology. Leake found him before he could escape back into battle, commiserating and cajoling. "You'll get one next time," he said, clapping Edmund on the back. "*Eagle*'s counting on you. The whole Navy's counting on you."

But time was running out. There would be two, perhaps three more sorties for Edmund before Force X detached and began to head back to Gib. His Hurricane was pushed aft, refuelled, had a cursory check for damage, and he was back on the treadmill. None of the pilots were exchanging words now. Their eyes were hollow, hands and arms limp. There were too many enemy aircraft. Just too many. They were ants against a stampede of elephants.

"Fighters from Sardinia are in range now, apparently," someone said, to be greeted with silence. "Macchis. And some of those new Reggiane kites."

Fighters. Now, when they were exhausted, their aircraft strained and battered. It was an epiphany. They were a sacrifice. No-one had a right to survive. More raids were called. The Hurricanes were readied and sent out again. They returned, most of them. Guns empty, propellant stains striping the wings, black oil bleeding from gaps in the cowlings. It was past eighteen-hundred, now. More raids were called. Brown Flight flew off, then Pink. Torpedo bombers on the port beam. White flew off, Lewis-Evans shot one down, damaged another. Past nineteen-hundred now, and *Cairo* reported a large group of aircraft fifty miles out, to the east.

There was nothing left. Nothing but to go up and fight - and keep going up. Past twenty-hundred now. Yeates' engine had been patched up. Yellow Section launched at twenty-twenty-two to join White. *In the order of fifteen aircraft at high altitude, twelve-thousand feet, one-zero-zero, buster, buster.*

Air under his wings at last. Edmund had been cut free. The Sea Hurricane was light under his hands. Its movements were delicate, precise. It would obey his will merely for the thinking of it, as his will was also the Hurricane's will. He glanced over towards Yeates, to share the joy, and saw Yeates' Hurricane amid billows of black smoke, already falling astern. Edmund thought he made out *"Engine packing up...throttling back..."* through the R/T - it was broken up, perhaps the Eyeties were jamming them - then he was alone, heading skywards, Tricky talking him onto White Flight, and then the raid.

There! Junkers, high above, two echelons of them, stacked up to starboard, pearl bellies against the blue deep. Edmund pulled the tit, overrode the boost control, asking everything of the Hurricane again. The three fighters stood on their tails, props scrabbling against the thinning air, yearning for the quarry.

In another instant, Edmund was aware of another presence, coming in from the beam. He hadn't been looking, it just snagged his peripheral vision, silvery like a school of fish in a tropical lagoon. Fighters. He called out the warning as they rolled over as one, glinting in unison, and carved downward in a Split-S. And for a moment, the two groups of fighters hurtled at each other, shimmering spider-silk trails lashing between them, twinkling lights of machine guns on wings and noses, closing, crossing.

One of the fighters hurtled beneath Edmund and he hauled the Hurricane into a bank, over the vertical and hard into the turn. *That was a Hurricane!* he thought, before checking himself, *don't be bloody stupid, where would a dozen Hurricanes come from at this altitude? Must be Reggianes.*

The airframe creaked and the stick bounced in his hands, the Hurricane curving downwards, gathering pace. A grey blizzard swarmed at the edges of his vision. Edmund had lost the fighter that had crossed with him, but another sheered across his path, in a climbing turn. He hauled the Hurricane round in pursuit, grey battering his vision again, darker, darker, and he thought he would black out altogether. But no, it was coming back the grey. The Reggiane was easing out of its turn and it swam across the reticle for a moment, just enough to loose off a few rounds, but the warning had been given and the Italian pulled into a tighter turn again.

The speed was coming off, scrubbed away by the friction of the turn. This was Hurricane territory. The Reggiane was faster, but Edmund was beginning to edge across its turn. Their turns were overlapping, Venn circles, and Edmund was a quarter behind, gradually, gradually pulling inside. Jesus, the Hurricane was horrible in this state. The turn was tight but imprecise. Invisible currents rippled against the fighter, jostling it. The Reggiane had the advantage, then Edmund did. They were balancing on their wingtips, locked in their circles, unstable as smoke, unyielding as steel. Tussling against themselves and their own aircraft for the tiny alteration that would mean life, death, spiralling gradually downwards as gravity demanded its tribute. They were passing through nine thousand feet. For a quarter of a second the Reggiane was in the sight, crossing the lead ring, and Christ, the controls were going mushy and damn it, damn it, the turn had been tightening and the Hurri was trying to swallow its own tail. Edmund pushed on the stick to stop it stalling and it was only a second but bugger it the Reggiane had crept ahead once more and he would have to do it all again. Eight thousand feet. Felt as though they had been grappling for hours.

He and the Reggiane were bound into the spiral, and as they curved round. Away from the wheeling scatter of other aircraft pursuing their own fights. And yet a fragment of consciousness remained of the other aeroplanes darting about outside the column of air circumscribed by Edmund and his Reggiane. It left Edmund with the increasing sense of the others gathering round to watch, like a fight in the schoolyard.

Dimly, Edmund became aware of voices in his ears. *Return to carrier...all aircraft return...break off Clyde, break off...fuel critical...*

The air was thickening, the turns tightening. Vapour streams poured off the Reggiane's wingtips, curling away under his Hurricane. And once again the machine was not just talking to him - but their thoughts had merged and he could play the pressure on the spade grip like a violin string, finding the frequency and balancing on a single, pure tone. The Reggiane was creeping up again in the reflector sight glass. He was finessing it towards the reticle, he would persuade it all the way through to the lead ring, and then his thumb would drop on the button and the tracers would arc out and burrow into the Reggiane in their fiery trails. Seven thousand feet.

Break off Yellow One...don't have the fuel...take him to the deck, the ack-ack will get him off you...return to ship now!

He shut the voices out. No. This was number five. This one would be his and he would earn it and everyone would leave him be.

The Reggiane buffeted on an unseen twist of air and he had another few yards. It would be soon. The moment would be soon. Perhaps the Italian had just tightened his turn too much as well, and had to back off. Edmund's shoulders strained at the harness straps. His arms were like iron rods. Six thousand. The fighter was through the sight now. Not far enough, but he was gaining. A little more. He tried a tentative half-second burst. The tracers hurled out, most of them went behind, a few striking and flashing on the tail. A few seconds more.

A bellowing silence, an odd feeling through the controls. The roar returned but the Reggiane was further away now. His engine spluttered, choking. It ran for another moment and then was silent. Fuel! Christ. Nothing. Empty. He caught one last glimpse of the Reggiane as it jinked and weaved, heading eastward, as he rolled the Hurricane level, shouting formless noise into his oxygen mask.

He was void. The next moments passed as if in a series of snapshots. Fragments, as if each were a chunk of a different life roughly edited together. In one, he glided the Hurricane back to the carrier and made a miraculous dead-stick landing. In the next, he piloted the aircraft to the sea and ditched gently upon it, sitting atop the fuselage until he was picked up. In the next, he bailed out and floated serenely down to plop into the ocean beside the planeguard destroyer. All of them happened - he lived happily ever after. None of them happened - they were patently ridiculous. He was dead. He just wouldn't be killed for a few moments more.

Mechanically, his hands pushed forward on the stick and felt the controls stiffening as the speed built. Now his hands were unlocking the canopy while his knees gripped the stick - and he heaved the frame back against the suction. His fingers pulled the pin from the Sutton harness, and the straps fell away. His eyes checked the ASI. His arms and feet smartly pushed the Hurricane into a roll, his brain counted to three, his hands shoving the Hurricane into a bunt, releasing the controls as his legs drew up to his chest and he was out of the Hurricane and into a hurricane.

There was a hurricane blasting past him. All around. His limbs were battered by it. There was no past or future. Just the gale blowing everywhere. Something tugged at his mind.

Le vent se lève. Il faut tenter de vivre.

He opened his eyes but his goggles had been ripped away. The wind screamed into his eyeballs and he slammed his eyelids shut. But in that instant, a realisation...the sky.

Il faut tenter de vivre... Il faut tenir la vie...

Try.

Hold on. Hold on.

He was falling through the sky. Panic erupted in his chest, his arms, his bladder, he flailed for the cord, almost hit the release, panicked again, found the cord. A kick across his whole torso. And the wind had calmed a touch while he was bouncing on an elastic band.

Le vent se lève.

The wind rises. We must try to live.

The sea was an obsidian slab beneath. Edmund had no idea how high he was. He could make out ships beneath, mostly by the faint glow of their wakes. For several minutes he didn't seem to be descending at all. Just stuck, like a fly in amber, swinging about beneath the chute.

And then he could hear the sea and make out the waves moving. The obsidian slab was rushing at him and-

An explosion of black cold, white stars. A strap around his chest, a great weight pushing him down, into himself, a fist, grasping, crushing, and more of the white star-shell flares, lightning, cannon fire. There was something he had to do but he couldn't focus. A pain built up, lancing into his chest-

It's because you're holding your breath - a voice said and he held the voice and considered it, as though it were made of glass. Five. Five was the important thing, but then it wasn't all that important after all. Something else, more pressing.

At that moment, the trough of a wave coincided with a gust of wind pulling on the parachute, and Edmund's head burst into the air for a second. He managed to suck in a bit of air, cough out a bit of water, hold his breath again before the next dunking.

He had rediscovered his hands. They flapped and scraped as he tried to move them. Parachute. Need to get out of the parachute. Fingers scrabbled on the metal disc on his chest, and

a thunk and the straps whipped away. His head went under again and he flailed his arms. They smashed on the black water. His mouth just above the surface, a tiny gulp of air, and then it was over his head again.

Sinking.

It was a pity. He caught a glimpse of distant ships processing by - and seemed to be watching both himself and the convoy. The man saturated, exhausted, sinking. The ships uncaring, implacable. The vision pulled outwards. Rommel and his hordes spilling over the frontier, overrunning Egypt. Mussolini reaching out toward Malta, with an arm made of Savoia-Marchettis, fingers that were Stukas.

There was something chafing against his neck. It seemed wrong to die with something impinging on his neck. He yanked at it. What was this? His Mae West, annoying bloody thing.

Sunrise revelation. Edmund groped for the flap. He could not pull against the resistance of the lever, and finally the CO2 canister *pfsssh*-ed - and the collar pressed on his neck. His head was a little further out of the water.

Hope had no time to return. He'd gone in near the front of the convoy, between columns, he realised. Low down as he was, the crawling lines of ships seemed to sit on each horizon. He could swim for hours and not reach them. Even if he managed to cover the distance, the convoy would be miles ahead by the time he got there.

There was the dye pouch, he supposed, but the ships so far distant would no more see that than the speck of a man's head.

What was the time? It would be dark before too long, the light was already beginning to fade. Should he leave it until morning? Maybe there'd be aircraft.

Morning! Ha! He'd never make it till morning. He found the dye patch, ripped it open. It felt like the thing to do. Might as well do everything he could. There was the light too, so he tripped that. And then it was in the lap of the gods.

Mercifully, there was no fear, no panic, no sudden turn to religion, no begging. He had already flung himself off the cliff face of life days before, and if he'd snagged on the rock of a petty concern, the superficial kindness of a stranger, it had not altered that fact. How ludicrous it all was. How little it should have meant to him, when he had the chance to confront it and dismiss it. It was too late now, but that was only a matter for passing regret. He had sacrificed a perfectly good Hurricane, and a pilot who...well, a pilot who at the very least could have helped break up and confound the raids on the convoy. And yet if it hadn't been for this fate, he wouldn't have realised. Everything that had happened was the only way it could have happened.

Darkness would fall. The convoy would press on. And that would be the end of it. A pity there would be no more chances. Life was not so generous.

He had comprehended Vickery's words. But too late. Vickery. Valéry. Of course. The journalist was an emissary from the poet. What a fool he had been. It seemed so obvious now.

Je suis en toi le secret changement.

The calm warmed his core, spread through his aching limbs as he slopped up and down on the waves. That was that. He'd done his best and had no more to give. The sea was purifying him. This surface was just a roof, white doves clinging to its glittering tiles, while beneath was a temple, dark, shaded, welcoming. He had used up what had made him himself, and was changing, ready for whatever came next.

I am what's secretly changing in you.

But something was impinging on the calm, and the change that it engendered. An irritation. A low, grumbling sound, accompanied by a harsh, hissing shush. And then an unearthly *woo-ip wooo-ip* shrieked out behind him and he sloshed himself round to see the knife-bows of a warship, huge, horrific, tearing down on him, full speed, hurling out a curtain of spray to either beam.

Courons à l'onde en rejaillir vivant.

Edmund watched in wonder as the vast ship shrank to a cruiser. And then again to a destroyer. After all this he was going to be run down by a ship. At least it would end quickly. The bow wave stretched out to either side of him, wings of an angel moulded from salt and spray.

Let's run to the wave to be hurled back to life

He would be hurled alright. The bow wave rose up before him, rushing to embrace.

And the destroyer was slewing away from him, slowing, the bow wave subsiding into a vast white churn around the vessel's waist. He looked up at the towering flank, bright grey, sailors clustering like beetles upon its decks and platforms. Aft of the waist, what he'd taken as camouflage was a vast patch of blackened, burned paint and soot. Heat-warped stanchions sprung out at hideous angles. Guns like spines jabbed at the sky.

A voice. A human voice, among the wind and the slosh of the waves and the growl of the engines. A bird-cry echoing down from the deck. It was a line, pulling him back into life. He could not fathom the meaning, but a line, a real one flicked out towards him, uncoiling, and whipped into the water. He threw an arm toward it, it didn't reach, threw another, paddled like a dog until he'd grasped the light cord with burning fingers. Through instinct rather than thought, he tied it under his arms.

The line jerked, bursting fire in his ribs.

Pulling him back to life.

He could not make out their voices, but Vickery's was in his mind - *try to live, try to live.*

And then he was slopping over the rail and onto the deck,

lungs full of flames and limbs full of acid. Hands were around him, living hands, bearing him up. And then they untied the line from around him and withdrew. He was released, and the grey blizzard around his vision swirled and the world vanished.

Part Two

Light seeped into Edmund's eyes again. Was it morning? He had something to do. He was flying at oh-eight-hundred-and-something...

Something was prodding at him.

"He's alive," a voice boomed. "Just passed out."

More things prodded at him, manoeuvred him, started pulling at his arms. He was borne up, and then the grey assailed him again and there was nothing to get hold of.

Edmund groped towards the light but the light seemed to be dimming again. Once again he was suspended in gloom, nothing above or below.

He had gone for his fifth. He had failed. He was still here. He clenched his hands, helpless, furious, squeezing until tears wrung beneath his eyelids. He'd have to do it all again. And yet here he was, stuck away from his squadron, his carrier, his aircraft. Embrace the failure. Wander. Die at some later date.

Or he could swim out of it. Fight now. Die now. As he had promised.

There was a third option. Something to do with... He heard Vickery's voice, distant, as if through water. He struggled towards it. Held the glass to the light.

Light. This time it was hard, white, sterile. He opened his eyes a crack, closed them, opened one.

"The airy-fairy's awake sir," a voice said too close, stinging his ears. He opened his eyes. White curtains, white painted decks and bulkheads. He was in a bunk with metal rails around it. Sick bay.

"Thanks," he said automatically to the rating who'd spoken when he'd recovered enough of his breath.

"Sir." The rating had not met his gaze, now turned away, attended to something else.

There was a polite theatre-cough and an "Excuse me" above him.

Edmund turned away from death to see an immaculately dressed RNVR lieutenant regarding him. For a moment he wondered if the man was real, or a vision.

"Sir," Edmund croaked. "Are you the surgeon?"

The officer laughed. "Good Lord no. Lieutenant Holdroyd, captain's secretary. I'm told you're alright, physically. Just had a bit of a shock, what with the tumble and the dunking. If you're up to it, would you be so good as to come this way? Captain Burgoyne would like to see you."

"Yes, of course," Edmund said, looking at his soaked and salt-rimed clothes, his skin stained with the dye and purple with cold. The officer did not offer a hand. He swung his legs over the edge of the bed, pushed himself to his feet almost toppled over with a punch of dizziness. But he recovered himself. When was it? What was happening with the convoy? "How long was I out?" was all he could find the words to ask.

"Only a quarter of an hour. As I said, you seem to be alright. You were lucky. We saw you come down, you fell an awfully long way before your parachute opened."

Ha! His vaunted luck again. "Yes. Lucky. Definitely." And thank Mac for packing his chute so well.

The officer led him out of the superstructure, forward, up zig-zagging decks and ladders until they stood on the tiny open bridge. The ship was minuscule. Was it even a destroyer? Edmund asked Holdroyd. The captain's secretary threw the answer over his shoulder - yes, HMS *Hindscarth*, a Hunt-class. An escort boat then. Holdroyd led him to a frowning three-striper who looked him up and down.

Edmund saluted. "Thank you for picking me up, sir."

The captain looked at Edmund's bare head, the sodden flying helmet grasped in his hand, and didn't return the salute. Regulations. "That's alright," he said. "Can't return you to your carrier though, I'm afraid. Force X is about to detach and we can't leave the convoy. You're with us to Malta, I'm afraid."

Though he was not sure why, Edmund felt a surge of relief, even exhilaration. *Eagle* would be heading back to Gib without him. Back towards safety. He was still with the convoy - and would sink or swim with it.

"Which ship were you with?" Burgoyne added.

"Oh, er, *Eagle*. Eight-Oh-One Squadron."

"Got that Holdroyd? We'll let them know we've got you. And your name?"

Blast, had he not introduced himself? He stammered out his rank and name.

The captain nodded almost imperceptibly. "Welcome aboard HMS *Hindscarth,* Acting Le'tenant."

"Oh I say!" the captain's secretary grinned. The captain glared at him, but he did not seem to notice. "Pardon me sir, but Lieutenant *Edmund* Clydesdale? The flying ace?"

He stared at Holdroyd. What on Earth? "Well I'm not an ace..." he stammered.

"Oh, don't be so modest! The chap who got the Vichy Frog plane in Madagascar last month? That was in the papers. Now I think of it, I recognise you from your photo."

"Er, yes, I suppose..."

The captain narrowed his eyes. "Didn't I hear that you were the highest scoring pilot out here? Your 'Wings' said something of the sort in Devonport."

Blast, would there be no respite from this? For this, he'd been dragged from the sea? The old world, the old life bustled back into his body. "That's right, sir. At least I was before we started, by now someone else might have-"

The captain was no longer listening. "Holdroyd, take the le'tenant below if you please. Oh, and make an announcement to the ship would you? There's a good chap. You never know, it might buck them up a bit to know there's an ace on board. Especially after the starboard Oerlikon."

"I'm not exactly... What happened to the starboard Oerlikon?" Edmund asked, reflexively stretching to peer over the rail at the gun, which stood idle on its platform, covers on, unmanned.

Holdroyd twisted his mouth irritably. "Oh, bad business. One of those Italian fighter chappies. Quarter of an hour or so ago. Came along and, what's the word? Strafed us. Treacherous little swine. Didn't do any damage but killed two men on the gun's crew."

"Oh. I'm sorry."

"*C'est la guerre*," he said in a monotone. "Now, if you'd come with me? I have my orders." Holdroyd threw a glance at the captain, who was deep in conversation with another officer. It seemed a moment about which things turned. He could spend the next day or two cowering in a warren of pipe-encrusted passageways, or he could act. He was free of everything that had dogged him since he first went into action. Here was a clean slate. He seemed to burn with the purity of it. By God, he wanted to be *doing* something. Protecting the convoy in any way possible. It might be a thimbleful to put out a forest fire, but he hadn't done enough, not nearly enough, when he had a Hurricane and eight machine guns at his disposal. He needed a chance to do something more.

"Is there anything I can do? Help with?"

The captain's secretary smiled awkwardly. "I don't suppose so. Though it's awfully kind of you to offer. Everyone has their role, you see. Train at it endlessly. Round the clock." He was almost hopping from one foot to the next.

Edmund thought of Vickery, tottering along under a pile of

mess tins. "There must be something."

Holdroyd pressed his lips together. "Please Lieutenant, I have to take you below. The captain will need me. What with being in the middle of a battle, and so on."

"But you're down a few men, you said. The fire party. And the starboard Oerlikon." The starboard Oerlikon. If there was one thing on this tub Edmund ought to be able to do, it was fire a machine gun at an aeroplane. And now there was no sense that he might be doing it for personal glory...to protect ships from bombs, torpedoes...

"Well, yes, but-"

"Excuse me Lieutenant." Edmund took a step back towards Burgoyne. "Captain, if I might have a quick word?"

The commander glared at his secretary, then turned to Edmund. "Rather busy at the moment, Acting Le'tenant."

"I know sir, I won't take up much of your time. It's just that I understand you can't man the starboard Oerlikon. No trained gunner, is that right? Well I'd like to volunteer." He could see the Captain was about to dismiss the idea. "I'm as qualified to shoot a gun at aeroplanes as any man, and more than most."

The Captain looked at Edmund in the kind of way he might if he'd suddenly realised he had met him before the war, and hadn't liked him then, either. Then he looked across at the empty starboard Oerlikon, and back at his secretary. "Have we crew to man it even with a gunner, Holdroyd? Wasn't just Moody, was it? I understand young Pelham bought it too."

"Yes, captain, and the reserve gunner died trying to put the fire out."

Fire? Edmund recalled the scorched and blackened splotch aft of the waist with a swooping sensation.

"Is there another loader? Oh, well, look into it and report back would you Holdroyd? I'd prefer it if we could man the gun all the same. You can make that announcement now. Thank you."

"Yes...I mean, aye aye sir." Holdroyd sketched the sloppiest salute Edmund had ever seen and took him by the elbow. "Persistent fellow aren't you?" the captain's secretary muttered through clenched teeth as they descended a short ladder aft of the bridge onto a platform before the funnel. "I suppose that's how you got all those Jerries, eh? Anyway."

Holdroyd nodded to the bosun's mate standing there. "Message for the crew. From the captain," he said, proud as any royal herald and rather more pleased with himself. The petty officer stepped up, bosun's call already at his lips, and piped into the loudspeaker attached to the bulkhead. The pipe shrilled through the tannoy, the speakers adding an edge to the sound. Holdroyd picked up the mouthpiece.

"Attention *Hindscarth*'s company. Lieutenant Holdroyd here. The captain wishes me to tell you that the airman we fished out of the drink just now is the famed flying ace Lieutenant Edmund Clydesdale, who shot down that Frog in Madagascar and has been in action against the German and Italian air forces today. Thanks to *Hindscarth* he can 'go up and fight, as the Lord commanded us' another day. That's all."

Edmund kept his head down, eyes on the deck. If the sailors reacted to the message, he didn't want to know. If they didn't react, that would almost be worse. As he looked up again he met the gaze of the port Oerlikon crew, standing around the gun, staring at him. He tried to smile - but failed and turned and looked to the other gun, which stood with its covers on, unmanned.

"Have you lost many?" Edmund said to Holdroyd. The platform felt horribly exposed. The only protection at all was a small splinter shield in front of the gun itself. The low bulwark wasn't even armoured.

"A fair few. When that fighter had a go at us. And the fire when a Junkers near-missed a while before that. Splinters, I gather, and something to do with oil lines. Horrible. *Hindscarth*'s been through it already."

No surprise about the looks he was getting. They didn't know he was a fraud. They just knew he hadn't protected their shipmates. Holdroyd picked up a speaking tube. "Damage control? Fore-bridge. Could you send Leading Seaman Carey up to the starboard Oerlikon? Thank you."

They moved across to the gun's platform and Edmund began to examine it. Looked straightforward enough. In a moment a short, broad-chested sailor - in his late thirties or early forties, Edmund estimated - appeared, saluted Holdroyd and glanced curiously at Edmund.

"Ah, Leading Seaman Carey," Holdroyd said. "This is Lieutenant Clydesdale. He's volunteered to act as gunner, and the captain agrees if we can fill the other posts."

The sailor beamed, showing a gap in his teeth. "Well that's fine, sir! Sillitoe can load."

That would have seemed to be that as far as Edmund was concerned, but Holdroyd knitted his brows. "Ah. Oh. There isn't anyone else? No-one at all?"

"Well, no sir. Sillitoe's your man. Bloody good...I mean to say, a very good loader. Experienced too, we were together on the *Exeter*."

"I don't know if the captain will like it."

"I'll keep him in line, sir. You won't regret it."

"What's the problem?" Edmund asked Holdroyd. "We can man the gun. What did this Sillitoe do that was so bad?"

He expected to hear of violence, insubordination, drunkenness, perhaps.

"Seaman Sillitoe has...a penchant for the theatrical," Holdroyd drawled. "Specifically, impressions."

Edmund felt laughter rising in his chest, forced it back. "Oh. And I suppose...?"

"The Captain was his most recent subject."

"Ah." Burgoyne struck him as a bit of a martinet. Probably abundant material for the ship's joker.

"Carey, would you find Lieutenant Clydesdale some dry clothes and look after him while we're at action stations?" the secretary said to the seaman, all charm and smiles once again. "Thank you."

"What did he do before the war?" Edmund hissed to Carey when Holdroyd had scampered back to the bridge.

Carey smirked. "Nobody knows for sure, sir, but the rumour is he was *maître d'* at the Ritz."

There was a brief, incomprehensible shout from the bridge, and a moment later, Holdroyd re-appeared.

"The captain begs me inform you that it's your job to keep him in line Lieutenant. And if he's any trouble he can go straight back to the mess party. So, it would be delightful if Sillitoe could be prevailed upon to restrain his performative tendencies for the remainder of the action. Given he'll only be a few feet from the bridge." Holdroyd inclined his head up, where the tops of the caps of the bridge officers could be seen, clearly in earshot, before excusing himself.

Carey regarded Edmund appraisingly. "Alright sir, shall we get you some dry kit and then we can sort this gun out?"

Edmund remembered with a jolt that he had not changed since he'd been dunked in the Med. He was also still clutching the salt-stiffened flying helmet. A sudden press of fatigue descended on him. He'd been flying all day and then in the sea. "Yes, thank you."

Once he was kitted out in dry slops and a tin helmet, they returned to the gun. Waiting there was a tall, rather gangling and boyish seaman who grinned sheepishly and turned his eyes to the deck. "Ordinary Seaman Sillitoe," the older sailor said. "He'll be your loader, sir."

The awkwardness of the two men was apparent. Edmund realised they weren't used to being under the direct command of an officer. No time to lose, though. He shucked off the tiredness, put it away. The sky was properly dark in the East now, and a deepening blue above. They'd been lucky in the half-hour since he'd been brought on board but there was still enough daylight for another raid. Carey told Edmund he'd better report that the gun was operational - and showed him how to use the speaking tube.

"Alright then gentlemen." He affected to sound breezy and realised he had failed when he heard the words coming out of his mouth. "Would you be so good as to explain to me how this contraption works? And I'll do my best to blow a few fascists out of the sky with it."

"Begging your pardon sir, but you've never fired a cannon before?"

For a moment Edmund thought he meant a Trafalgar-era muzzle-loader. "Yes, I have," he said, quickly masking his look of puzzlement. "Though not one that wasn't stuck to an aeroplane." Even that was spinning more cloth than the thin thread of truth should allow. He'd fired a Hurricane IIC's Hispano 20mm in the butts once or twice in Egypt. Never an Oerlikon. But that was more or less the same wasn't it? He saw the quiet, respectful horror on their faces. Seaman Moody had been a virtuoso on the twenty mil cannon, by the sound of things. The honour of the starboard Oerlikon was at stake. And there was a danger that he might hit some other part of the ship, or another ship, or a friendly aircraft. Damn, what was he doing?

Something. He was doing something.

Try to live. Not just to live. *Try*.

"...But rest assured that I've fired plenty of automatic guns at plenty of aeroplanes, and I'll do my best."

Carey nodded, though his frown had not entirely disappeared.

"Alright sir. Well." He removed his tin hat, scratched his forehead and scrunched his face up for a moment. "It's dead simple really. As gunner, you just lean your shoulders into the rests here..." He patted the U-shaped bars at the back of the gun. "And hold the grips here. The trigger's on the right hand grip. It's in 'safe' at the moment."

Edmund stepped forward and leaned into the gun. Everything fell easily to hand.

Carey nodded. "That's it sir. Why not swing it about a bit, get a feel for it?"

Edmund did as he was told. The grips were like bicycle handlebars. He kept his hand well away from the trigger. The gun traversed smoothly. It wasn't difficult to move in the slightest. He tried changing the elevation, up and down. To his surprise, the barrel whipped almost to the maximum. It took no pressure at all. He exclaimed. "It's light, isn't it?"

"There's a spring in the mount counterbalancing everything. And the bearings are nice and smooth. We keep them well oiled. Obviously."

"I see." There was an eyepiece to the right of the breech with a glass lens in it, and on a bracket, a metal ring with smaller concentric rings within it, ten spokes radiating from inner ring to outer, and a cross in the middle. Seemed simple enough. "Gunsight here, anything I need to know about that?"

"No, it's fixed and all a bit on the basic side. Lead will vary with speed, size and distance, you just need to get used to it really. I can adjust it a bit so it's a bit more comfortable." Carey unscrewed a knob on the sight mounting and swivelled it until Edmund could see straight through without craning.

"Alright. Operation?"

"That's simple too. Hardly any moving parts. To start with, pull the breech block back. Like this. And then it's ready. Set the trigger lever to 'fire'. Like this. And then pull the trigger.

Simple as that. Then to 'safe' again when you're done."

"What's the rate of fire?"

Carey scrunched his face again. "Four hundred and fifty is the maximum. In practice we don't get as much of course."

"How much does a drum hold?"

"Sixty rounds."

Edmund whistled. "So you need to change drum every...what? Seven and a half seconds!"

Carey smiled tightly. "Only if you fire continuously, sir."

"Yes. Right." Edmund nodded, but even if he was cautious, it would mean no more than two bursts, three if he kept them shortish, before the drum needed changing.

"And as for that," Carey went on, "when a drum's finished, the trigger will return to the checked position and you won't be able to pull it. Stick your hand up, and Sillitoe will change the drum - although usually he's pretty good at spotting when the gun's empty and will be on his way. He'll be standing behind and to the right. Don't worry about him when you're swinging the gun about, he'll get out of the way."

"Right. And what will you be doing?"

"I'll be keeping an eye out for raids, and spotting for you. And handing Sillitoe new drums and taking the old ones. Here's how it works." The two seamen moved into position, either side of the barrel. Sillitoe took off the drum and placed it on the deck, while Carey handed a new one over the barrel to him. In a practised movement, Sillitoe got it seated with a metallic snap, picked up the old drum and stepped back. The whole thing had taken perhaps seven or eight seconds.

"I see. I imagine it gets rather busy."

"You could say that, sir, yes. Oh, and when an attack starts, the captain tends to turn into it. Just so's you're aware."

Another factor to try and incorporate into the calculations that were pinging through his brain. Edmund nodded slowly, running through it all. "Strap me in, will you? I ought to try to get as much of a feel for it as possible before the next raid turns up."

"Right you are sir. And sir?"

"Yes?" Edmund disengaged himself from the gunsight and turned to face Carey.

"You don't need to shoot them down. Just give the buggers a bit of a scare."

He pursed his lips and nodded once. "Understood."

"It would be nice if you could shoot a few down though," Sillitoe broke in. "I've a bet with the pom-pom lads."

Carey let his head tip forward into his hands. "Bloody hell Dicey, how much have you taken us for?"

"Got an ace at the gun, ain't we?" Sillitoe jerked his head at Edmund.

"For God's sake will everyone stop saying that!" Edmund exploded. "I'm not an ace. I'm not a bloody ace! An ace has got five kills, and I haven't!"

"Sorry sir, sorry!" Sillitoe patted the air in placation. "I just thought Prissy Holdroyd said-"

"Le'tenant Holdroyd..." Edmund realised how shrill his voice was, looked around sharply in case anyone on the bridge had heard. "The captain's secretary doesn't know...his ace from his elbow."

The two seamen smirked to each other. "So how many kills have you got then sir?" Sillitoe said after a moment. Edmund tried not to roll his eyes. What did the man want, an autograph? No, wait - he was just wondering how much money he was going to lose.

"Four."

"Oh, well, just need one more then." Sillitoe's grin returned instantaneously.

Christ, why had he said that? It was really one and a couple of 'damaged'. Not that his 'official' score wasn't well enough publicised.

Was everyone in this bloody war obsessed with how many kills he could bag?

"The pom-pom has four barrels and twice our range," Edmund sighed. "And I don't intend to compete with them. We've our own job to do, let's just get on with it, alright?"

"Aye, sir." Sillitoe winked ostentatiously.

Edmund familiarised himself as best he could with the operation of the gun, and the feel of it. Perhaps when things got going, it wouldn't be so much different from aerial combat. Maybe it would even be easier. There were fewer variables, after all. He tried out different ways of moving himself at different angles of the gun. At high elevations, he decided it was better to let his feet slide forwards and to hang off the straps than to squat. After a while, he felt there was no sense in tiring himself out any more. He'd learn no more until they were under attack. Carey unstrapped him, he stretched, and leaned against the bulkhead.

"Now we wait, I suppose?"

"That's right. A lot of it's waiting, even when we're under attack, believe it or not. Takes a while before anything gets within range of this peashooter. Four thousand yards, though you won't hit much even at that distance. There's no point blasting away before they get close."

Darkness was falling. That didn't mean there would be no more raids. But every moment less of daylight meant it was less likely a raid would have set out, still less likely they would be able to bomb accurately. "Better do this while there's still some light," Sillitoe said and began to load up empty drums, whistling as he greased rounds from a case and snapping them into the metal snailshell of the magazine. The eastern sky was already a deep blue, turning indigo, and the western sky began to follow.

After a while, there was only the faintest pale streak to remind them that the sun had been up at all. The ship was silent, efficient. While he had been practising with the gun, *Hindscarth* had re-taken its place in the screen, and there were other small destroyers, similarly silent, similarly warlike, scything along in a line beside them. More 'Hunts', Edmund supposed. Everyone was still at their action stations. The mess party came round with cocoa. The convoy made a few course adjustments. Finally, it seemed as though nothing would happen until morning.

Just then, a sort of thickness started to intrude into the air. Edmund examined it.

"Listen," he said. "Aircraft." He tried to fasten on it, but once he knew it was there it was harder to pin down. And then the *thff-thff-thff* of distant ack-ack from the other side of the fleet started up, and the aircraft could not be heard any more. Carey and Sillitoe had stiffened, their fingers all but twitching in anticipation of the job to come. Edmund smiled. "I'm fairly certain those were ours. They didn't sound like Jerries, at any rate. Wellingtons, perhaps? No, Beaufighters, I dare say."

"But they're shooting at them," Carey said, "so they can't be ours can they?"

It was all Edmund could do not to bark with laughter. "Shall I tell you how many times the convoy shot at me?"

Carey looked crestfallen at that. Edmund softened his expression. "It's understandable. Shoot first and ask questions later. And this is the first time we've managed to bring a proper air group to cover a convoy from the air. They...you just aren't used to seeing friendly aeroplanes. But Lord knows there are few enough of them, the least we can do is try not to hit our own machines."

Carey nodded, placated. Sillitoe looked thoughtful. "It would be just like those bastards on the pom-pom to knock down a couple of ours just to win the bet. I'd better tell 'em that won't count."

It wasn't certain, of course, that the aircraft was friendly. That was for sure. Edmund realised he'd never heard a Savoia-Marchetti, and for all he knew their engines were synchronised like on British aircraft, and they sounded similar. In theory friendly aircraft should be able to communicate with *Cairo*, the fighter control cruiser, but in reality? There were all manner of cock-ups that could prevent the aircraft from talking to the ships.

Ten or fifteen minutes later, the loudspeaker squealed, and Holdroyd's voice cut through the evening calm. "Lieutenant Holdroyd here. I'm informed to tell you that some of our fighters from Malta report that the Italian fleet is out. We'll likely meet them some time in the morning watch."

Carey issued a low whistle. Everyone else stayed quiet. Edmund felt his stomach give a lurch. The Italian fleet? Did that include battleships? He'd expected aircraft. That was one thing. But to get into a sea battle as well? Oh, good heavens above.

It occurred to him that Vickery would probably give his right arm to change places with him now. The thought spurred a wan smile. At least he'd witness something worth seeing. He slipped into a reverie as the night wore on, though he tried to keep one ear out for torpedo boats. The Oerlikon would probably be the best defence against something like that.

"They'll probably head back in rather than engage," Edmund said, echoing the Commander Flying's words, more in hope than expectation. "Isn't that what they usually do?"

"They fought a bit at Sirte," Carey said. "Didn't put up too much of a fight, but they kept us out another day and then their aircraft hit the merchantmen before they could unload."

"Oh."

"Jesus, what's that?" Carey breathed, peering over Edmund's shoulder and cutting across his thoughts.

Edmund whipped around. Two lights had appeared in the sky, flaring yellow-white. Shooting stars? No, don't be silly. They were descending gradually, their brilliance flickering but not fading.

"Parachute flares," he answered. They were a good few miles away but a watery gleam was clearly visible off the sea around them. The ships of the convoy, totally invisible a moment before, were now made plain, like cardboard cut-outs against the backdrop of the night. "Eyeties looking for us."

"The whole Fleet's lit up!" Sillitoe slurred. "When I say 'lit up', I mean lit up...by fairy lamps!"

The gun crew chortled, the tension vanished, for a moment anyway. It could have been Thomas Woodrooffe himself standing next to them. Edmund felt a sharp swipe of longing. He'd listened to that Coronation Fleet Review broadcast with his Dad and they'd been helpless with laughter by the time the producer had pulled the plug on the drunk presenter. Seemed a long time ago now

"The whole fleet is in fairyland! There's nothing, nothing between us and heaven," Sillitoe intoned.

"Whoever that is, bloody shut it," hissed out of the darkness from the direction of the bridge.

Sillitoe stopped and the rest of them did their best to muffle the laughter with their sleeves. After a moment, Sillitoe, still in Woodrooffe's voice, sotto voce, could be heard uttering "I'm sorry, I was just telling some people to shut up talking," which set them all off once again.

The flares continued sinking, and eventually blinked out. "Other side of Zembra," Carey whispered. "They must think we're sticking to seaward. Could be a signal to their destroyers do you think, sir?"

"Doubt it," Edmund replied. "They'd want us lit up, not them."

"...By fairy lamps..."

"Shhh!"

Edmund listened for aircraft. There must be one up there, but it must have been high, or even further away than he thought. It was as though the flares had appeared out of nowhere, and as he ruminated, one guttered out, then the other, and it was as though they had existed in a moment isolated from everything else. Perhaps more would appear at any moment, right above them. The time ticked on. There were no more flares. It made little sense. Nothing seemed to make any sense any more. Half an hour later they heard gunfire off to the front of the convoy. The men sprang to immediate alertness and Edmund strapped into the gun. Maybe there was a torpedo boat attack. But the guns fell silent, and *Hindscarth* kept ploughing on into the night. A little later, there seemed to be some flashing lights in the sky over Cap Bon, and once again they readied themselves. But the signals, if they were signals, did not bring some new enemy down on them.

The night passed thus, as if they convoy were passing into Virgil's underworld. There would be no aircraft, but a raid by those fast Eyetie torpedo boats could be on them almost without warning. Torpedoes slamming into the flank from a submarine would come with no warning at all. Eventually Edmund's fear seemed to use itself up, and he began to understand the stoic courage of those around him. You could either find it or drive yourself mad.

The three men on the gun took turns staying alert, allowing the others to doze a little, though nobody really slept. A couple of times in the night cocoa, tea and biscuit was brought round to men at their stations. Gradually, Edmund lost all sense of time.

DAY 3

15 June 1942

And then it was morning. The world of black lit only by gleams miraculously transformed into a sludgy grey of almost no light at all, and then the salmon glow on the eastern horizon.

Sunrise was a quarter to five. It was a way off yet. Edmund ran through some calculations. Assuming the first raid of the day took off from Sicily in darkness, and did not have to spend much time looking for them, they could be under attack by ten past six, give or take a few minutes. With any luck they'd be properly under Malta's fighter umbrella by then, at least the outer fringe of it. He made sure to stretch thoroughly, pissed in a scupper, and when the time came, he had Carey strap him back in to the Oerlikon.

Sure enough, the sun had not been long over the horizon when Carey tap-tap-tapped on his tin hat and jabbed his arm. Two elongated blobs in a shallow dive, at about five hundred feet, heading right up the middle column of the convoy. Edmund swung the gun, lined up the sight...and then held his arm up. "They're Beaufighters!" he shouted at Carey, a moment before the pom-pom began to blast away at the fighters. "Tell Guns, will you."

Carey dashed to the speaking tube and few seconds later the pom-pom fell silent. "That was lucky," the seaman said when he'd regained his station.

"Luck, bollocks," Edmund spat. "It was good aircraft recognition. This convoy's recognition is bloody terrible."

"Aye sir, sorry sir."

The fighters finished their 'beat-up' of the convoy and pulled into a steep climb, heading out of view. A few minutes later, he spotted them again, orbiting lazily, buzzards in a thermal, ahead of the convoy. His heart lurched in his ribcage but a second glance all but confirmed it. Beaufighters. Bloody marvellous!

They were properly under Malta's protection now.

What came next was not bloody marvellous.

"Attention on deck," Squealed out from the loudspeakers, in the offhand BBC-announcer voice of the Captain's secretary. "Aerial reconnaissance has reported Italian warships - cruisers and destroyers - around 15 miles on our port beam. I'm to tell you that we'll be going into action with them before long. Good luck to us all."

"Jesus," Edmund breathed.

"That's torn it," Carey said.

"This is a g-gwave hour, the most fuh-fateful in our...ah-histowy," said the voice of King George VI behind them.

"Stow it, Sillitoe," Carey, muttered.

"Perhaps leave Le'tenant Commander Woodrooffe out of it as well today, eh Sillitoe?" Edmund added. The fleet would likely be lit up soon enough alright, and not with fairy lamps.

"Aye aye sir," Sillitoe's voice caught and Edmund realised for the first time why the seaman did what he did.

Edmund forced himself to smile. "I don't know, can't you give us a George Formby once in a while? Laurence Olivier, someone like that?"

Sillitoe looked hurt and then indignant, before the usual grin broke out again. "Well where's the fun in that sir? George Formby don't have the power of life and death over us."

Edmund peered at the seaman with an eyebrow raised. "I hope for your sake it's still the King in charge when we get to Malta and not Mussolini."

"Oh, me too, sir," Sillitoe said, cheerily.

The deck beneath their feet started to vibrate and Edmund could tell they were working up to high speed. The air filled with the tang of oil fuel and salt. The bow wave began to hiss more insistently, and diamonds of spray blew back on the wind. For ten minutes, the destroyers accelerated.

This was serious, then. In a kind of rude, mechanical ballet, the destroyers fell out of line abreast and into line astern, *Hindscarth* slotting into second place. A bigger ship, the cruiser, *Cairo*, fell in ahead of them. Another line of warships was forming ahead and to starboard - they looked like larger destroyers, which began to race ahead. In another few minutes, Carey cried "look!" and pointed. With the destroyer's pitching, and all the spray it was throwing up, it was hard to make out at first, but then Edmund's eyes adjusted and he saw a row of dark marks against the horizon, tiny diagonal barbs like the blades of a saw. Five...six...seven?

Bloody hell. Warships. He hoped that one day someone would explain to old Leaky on *Eagle* that the Italians had not put their heads out of port and straight back in again this time. Whatever the outcome, it would not be him that put 'Wings' straight on the matter.

Just then a white pillar burst out of the sea between them and distant smoke-smudges. It shot up to a ragged point, then collapsed gracefully like a falling chimney. Edmund felt a swirl of outrage. *Those bastards are shooting at me! How dare they!* His hands gripped tighter on the handles, and he smiled grimly to recall the very same sentiment that had struck him the first time he experienced return fire from a Jerry bomber.

"Short," Carey murmured.

"Language!" Sillitoe said.

"I said..." Carey grinned and shook his head. "It's lucky you can load."

"So, what happens now?" Edmund tried to keep the panic out of his voice. There was bugger all they could do against cruisers with this pop-gun and they were completely exposed to shellfire, splinters, fire...

Carey shrugged. "Sit back and watch. We've got the best seats in the house." Edmund's face must have registered the horror he felt, as the seaman cracked a smile and added "It's the fleet destroyers that'll go for the Eyeties, we'll most likely be trying to keep between them and the convoy with the other Hunts."

"Language!" Sillitoe whooped with faux outrage.

"Oh, put a sock in it," Carey snapped, though he was smiling as he said it. "And if we do fight, we'll have a nice thick smokescreen to dive in and out of. It'll be all right sir. Makes a change from all those bloody aeroplanes, anyway."

That was one way of putting it.

Another crystal pillar thrust out of the sea, and an instant later another two, three, close to it, and melted, sloshing into the waves. As if the shellfire was a signal, Cairo, ahead leaned over and turned hard to port. When *Hindscarth* reached the churning angle in the wake, the deck slanted, and the destroyer began to sheer around, until it was cutting across the path of the convoy, between it and the enemy. Edmund watched in wonder as a thrust of oily black burst from *Cairo*'s funnels, and for a second he thought she must have blown up her engines. Then he remembered the smokescreen Carey had mentioned. He turned to *Hindscarth*'s funnel, just behind them and saw an identical pall, so thick it seemed almost solid, thundering into the air, then curling downward and twisting flabbily over the surface of the sea. *Cairo*'s smoke, stodgy, insoluble, merged with *Hindscarth*'s as the destroyer advanced, and then with the other destroyers astern. In an instant the Italian ships on the horizon were obscured behind a dense hedge of smoke.

"Convoy's turning back," Carey said, and pointed ahead. Edmund leaned over the rail and peered past the bridge superstucture. It was true. The merchantmen and the minesweepers, all their remaining protection, had their sterns to him. Bloody hell.

"After all this!" Edmund cried. "Everything we've done, and they're going back to Gib!" It was incomprehensible.

"Maybe not," Carey replied. "Might just be putting a bit of space between them and the Eyeties." He didn't sound convinced.

Christ.

The destroyers continued laying their smokescreen. Somewhere beyond it, the fleet destroyers were charging towards the enemy. *Hindscarth* thundered on, now at top speed, and her stern seemed to squat down, a plume of white water gushing aft from the bow. *Cairo* turned hard to starboard and was gone beyond the smokescreen in seconds. The deck shifted again. *Hindscarth*, now in the lead, sheered to port, and Edmund braced his feet against the painted steel. He could not make out what was happening, but from a rough estimate of their course, they were trying to lay smoke around the east and north of the merchant ships.

The smoke from the funnel thinned, and in a moment was the usual faint brown wisp, the air seeming to clear with it. *Hindscarth* turned port yet again, and he could see all the destroyers were hauling round in a tight half-circle, so they were now last in line. For a minute, two, the destroyers hurtled back the way they had come, parallel to the smoke barrier that hid everything to the east and south.

"Might want to take a breath, sir," Carey said, nodding at the smokescreen. As if in response, Hindscarth heeled again and a moment later they plunged into dense oily fog.

In that instant, the sun was gone and Edmund could see no further than the railing around the Oerlikon. The back of his throat, and eyes stung. He was trying to breathe as little as possible but there was no air and he kept heaving the black clag into his lungs. He held his sleeve over his nose, but it did no good.

And blessed miracle, they were out again, into clear, bright air. Edmund's lungs felt as though they were full of glue, his eyes full of soap.

"Blow me, would you look at that!" Sillitoe was jabbing his finger dead ahead. Edmund had to blink violently, trying to flood his eyes with tears, and then wipe them away and-

Christ! Two Italian destroyers, a few thousand yards away, crossing their course. Edmund's mouth fell open. Enemy warships, just...there! He tensed his muscles waiting for the shells that must pile into the destroyer in the next seconds.

Hindscarth turned yet again, leaning like a motorbike, presenting her starboard flank to the ships even as her rail dipped into the swirling waters. Edmund cringed away, but he was strapped into the gun. He felt a momentary stab of fury, and it took all his resolve not to start shooting the Oerlikon, with its tiny twenty-millimetre shells, at the enemy warships.

But someone was firing. The four inch guns ahead and behind roared out almost as one, stabbing tongues of flame at the Eyeties. This was more like it! The guns fired again, and then a vast *wooooosh!* next to them, the world disappeared in a welter of white, and Edmund was soaked to the bone in the blink of an eye.

"Close," Carey murmured conversationally, and Edmund stared at him, eyes like caverns. "Oh, they're turning away."

Edmund turned to look but *Hindscarth* fired again, and again, and was then turning herself, back into the smoke, and the world was once again choking him. A few moments later they peeked out, to find the Italian destroyers had reversed course, heading back for the main body of their ships. The British destroyers dipped behind the smoke once more and headed south. There were whoops and cheers that they'd seen off the Eyeties with half a dozen salvos, but then the other destroyers were seen turning again, once more trying to work around the end of the smoke. Another few salvos from the main guns of the four British destroyers, and the enemy ships were end-on, opening

the distance. Edmund felt a tightness in his chest and realised he was holding his breath - whether from the smoke or the tension of the battle, he could not be sure.

He looked back towards the merchantmen, now tiny and partially hull-down. Oh no. No! The air above the ships was thick with ack-ack blasts, and tiny black motes moved among the barrage. "Look!" he yelled, jabbing his finger, even as a cluster of water columns burst among the ships, sending silent spray high into the air. "Stukas!"

"I know, sir," Carey said sadly. "They pull the escort away with their cruisers and then hit the transports with their planes. Nothing we can do."

Edmund snarled, shook his head, as if to dislodge the unwelcome thoughts. Cheating swine! Cowards. *Come over here and fight us!* he wanted to scream.

The fleets jockeyed, firing, withdrawing briefly, advancing once again and exchanging deafening salvos. In just over an hour, the Italian warships were smudges on the horizon again, blessed miracle, and the merchant ships had turned back towards Malta. All the British escorts were back together. Most of them, at any rate. There were only three fleet destroyers. And *Cairo* had a huge hole blown in her superstructure, the scorching of paint and propellant all over her topsides.

"Looks as though *Bedouin* and *Partridge* copped it," Carey said grimly, as he counted along the remaining vessels.

"Do you think they'll be back?" Edmund asked.

"No idea sir. But *they* will be." The seaman pointed his arm over Edmund's head and shouted in his ear. "Your turn now. There!"

And there they were, a string of beads moving obliquely across the sky in echelon starboard. Here it was. After all this. It just came down to him and this gun. Edmund gave the thumbs up without speaking. As he did so the sky erupted in an epidemic of black detonations, turning a layer of the air into a mesh. Aft of the funnel, the pom-pom bellowed out with its syncopated *thmp, thmp, thu-thmp, thu-thmp*, and a moment later the four-inchers joined in, booming, until there were no individual sounds, just a constant waterfall din.

Overhead, the string was unperturbed. The mesh thickened, grew more violent, seeming to stitch itself into the sky and evaporate while being renewed with new stitches. The mesh would never be thick enough. The string of beads kept on, not deflected even slightly from their grotesque progression.

Leave us alone! screamed silently in Edmund's head. *Leave us and go for the convoy! Look, there! Those fat, wallowing cargo ships!*

If Edmund could have taken his tin hat off in the middle of an air raid and bashed himself over the head with it, he would have. Instead, he started tracking the aircraft through the gunsight, though they were far out of range. Ignore that, he thought to himself. *Come here, you bastards, and let's see how you like the taste of twenty mil cannonfire.* He already knew from something about the way they moved, approached...the speed, perhaps, or the attitude...that they were Junkers Eighty-Seven 'Stukas'. Not nearly such a big bomb load as an Eighty-Eight but quite enough to blow the bottom out of a tub like this, and a damn sight more accurate.

They'd be going for the convoy, wouldn't they? Not the escorts? And yet all yesterday the bombers had been driving at the escorts, wave after wave of them, trying to take out the aircraft carriers. Here they came, still. All that AA fire in the air, and not one bit of shrapnel had hit one aircraft somewhere important? It was insulting.

Still they came.

They were overhead now, right overhead, and just as Edmund had convinced himself they were passing the destroyers to hit the merchant ships, they seemed to hesitate, and then, one by one, the beads began slipping off the string and falling, falling...

"Remember the Captain'll turn in!" Carey yelled in his ear. Edmund nodded once, not taking his eyes off the Stukas for an instant. The relative movement of the beads began to slow and then, by Jesus, they were barely moving at all. *Coming for us*, Edmund thought, and this time there was no panic, no fear. He lined up the cross on what he took to be the leading Stuka, but they were all overlapping now. Beads turning to stunted crosses, long in the arms, short in the upright, and a moment later, not crosses but the shrugging gull-wing. Wait for it...wait for it... He steadied the sight on that almost stationary form. And then the deck tilted under his feet, the Stukas wandering out of the cross-hairs. Damn it! But something had taken over. He was no longer calculating, but just feeling. Sensing the movement of the ship through the soles of his shoes, the movement of the aircraft. It was too late for them to correct.

"You should have stayed at home, you bastard," he muttered and pressed the trigger. Edmund didn't even feel the recoil pulsing into his shoulders this time, didn't register the puffs of smoke from the barrel. Just the flares of tracer curving on their mathematical path, physics dictating their destiny, and he was still feeling. Tracers were fluttering around the nose of the Stuka and he was no longer aware of any movement of ship or aeroplane. It was as though he had lassoed the Stuka and he was hanging onto it despite everything it could do to escape. Black puffs started appearing in his sights - later he'd realise it was the pom-pom aft finding the range too - and the tracers were flashing, flaring. The Stuka began to wander downwards out of the sight, flickering with an odd light. Disinterested, Edmund held fire, a part of his brain he was not fully aware of realising that the aircraft could no longer hit the ships and was no longer important. He found another target and began painting it with tracers just as he had the first. Then, with a clunk, the trigger snapped open. The magazine had run out. He started to raise his arm but Sillitoe had already leant in and was snapping the clasps open - and there was Carey on the left with a new magazine. Seconds ticked by, feeling like minutes. And then the gun was back together and the next wave was coming in and the tracers were looping out to meet them...

Not for the first time over the last few days, Edmund lost all sense of time. Existence telescoped into a kaleidoscope of onrushing aircraft that might have been an instant or an eternity. A wave of Junkers Eighty-Eights in their typical thirty degree dive, sticks of bombs peeling away as they pulled up. Wave-hopping Savoia-Marchetti Seventy-Nines dashing in - like small packs like bandits or wild dogs, dropping torpedoes and dashing away. Edmund blasted away at a Seventy-Nine, seemingly pouring rounds into the centre engine...he felt he could have made out the colour of the pilot's eyes...and then he was swinging his gun, looking to Carey to point out the next threat, only to find there was none.

The speaking tube whistled. Carey picked it up. "Starboard Oerlikon...no more raids on the plot...understood." He turned to Edmund and Sillitoe, pushing his tin hat back and wiping his brow. "Scope's clear for the time being. We can relax a bit."

"How're you finding the cannon then sir?" Sillitoe asked, as if he were asking Edmund about a new car or a pair of shoes. "Reckon it might be good for your fifth kill?"

"I don't even have four kills," Edmund wailed, before he could stop himself. "The first one, alright, that one I shot down though it was just blind luck that a Jerry overshot. The others at best count as 'damaged'. Maybe one or two are 'probable' if you are in a generous mood. I'm nothing special! I'm not even any good!"

Carey and Sillitoe gaped at him, though whether it was due to seeing an outburst of weakness from an officer or the shock of realising their gunner was a fraud, he could not tell. Carey opened his mouth as if to speak, and then the speaking tube whistled again, and the leading seaman went to it.

"Another formation inbound. Low level, five miles, south east."

"Alright then," Edmund said, apprehension at the raid and relief at the interruption warring within him. He reset the breech block, just to be sure, and aimed the barrel roughly where he expected the raid to come from. In a moment, the aircraft were visible, a row of them across the horizon, each just a dash against the sky but already unmistakable in the way they thickened slightly in the middle as Savoias. They came on, and on, and on, splitting up, jinking, heading for different targets. One of them had no lateral movement at all...even with the motion of the ship, this aircraft was locked onto them. Bastard. Just get in a bit closer, Edmund thought, just a bit more, and you'll regret getting out of bed this morning...

"Torpedo!"

The alarm sounded and the deck slanted beneath his feet. Even strapped into the Oerlikon, Edmund almost lost his footing. And then, as the view around the bulkhead panned round to port, he saw it. The torpedo bomber, a Savoia Seventy-Nine, struggling to gain height, to turn. It presented its entire topside to him as he trained the gun.

He slewed the barrel and felt once again the mathematical arcs of ship and aircraft and cannon round and air, even with the destroyer slewing beneath his feet, the aircraft curving, it was as though he were isolated in space, swinging the Savoia on the end of a rope. The tracers bowled out, up, and seemed to draw down towards the aeroplane by a kind of magnetism, gravity turned sideways. Flash, flash, flash on the fuselage, around the cockpit, as though they were signalling, stop! stop! *No*, he responded, keeping the rope taut, the tracers hurling at the machine, battering at it.

By then it seemed as though every gun in the convoy must have been trained on the Savoia. Shrapnel blasts pocked the air around it, splashes like rain on a puddle churned the water beneath. The Seventy-Nine began to sink, seemed to skim the waves then swooped back upward, gaining a hundred feet, two... But a dirty trail was marking its course, and then a lurid match-flare glowed within it, rushing from front to back, and then the bomber was sinking, brushing the sea like a skipped stone, then a bursting haemorrhage of spray and it was down. Reduced to a scatter of litter. Gone.

"Jesus!" Edmund muttered. Sillitoe and Carey were laughing, shouting insults and whoops of triumph at the patch of scattered debris on the water, which calmed and drew back together, as if a moment of violence and death had never marred it.

There were more moments of relative calm. And more of howling aircraft, thundering guns, fire and death. The day wore on, into the afternoon and early evening. Dribs and drabs of information came through. HMS *Bedouin* had been sunk after a long effort to save her. A couple of merchantmen had been torpedoed. The deck was thick with spent shell-casings that tinkled like a glockenspiel when the ship rolled. There was a stack of empty magazines three feet high in the corner of the platform. The paintwork was pitted and scored by burnt propellant. Carey told them there was another big raid coming in. *Cairo*'s scope was thick with plots. They were perhaps three hours from Malta. Just three hours. There were two merchant ships remaining. Two, out of six that had left Gibraltar.

And there were the aircraft coming in. Rows of them, just marks against the sky, each no bigger than a full stop. Each one a Junkers Eighty-Eight, dipping into a dive, running straight at them. Edmund's hands were claws, frozen around the grips. He readied the gun again, focussing on the dots as they grew and grew, each budding wings, engines, tails...

And from above them, more motes were coming in, barrelling down, slashing across the formations, streaks of smoke pencilling the air, wheeling around, scything back in. Their tracers painted the sky red. The groups of Junkers were splintering, dissolving.

"Here comes the cavalry!" Edmund yelled. "Spitfires! Spits from Malta! Bloody marvellous!"

"Cor, blimey," Carey whistled. "Look at 'em go."

"No magician who ever could have waved his wand could have waved it with more acumen," Sillitoe drawled. Edmund was too tired to laugh, but he mustered a wan smile.

The Spitfires carved and wheeled through the bombers, shattering them, smoking with bloody execution. Only a few bombs fell near the convoy. Half a dozen Junkers joined them in the churning waters.

At around dusk, the silhouette of an island was visible against the fading sky, and soon the remaining ships were creeping into the swept channel, then anchoring in the harbour. Commander Burgoyne thanked Edmund cursorily, Holdroyd shook his hand, Sillitoe gave him a few more words of Thomas Woodrooffe's slurring broadcast, and Leading Seaman Carey volunteered for the boat crew that would row Edmund ashore. As he drew away from the little destroyer, he felt a pang. And a fierce desire to get into a Hurricane again and fight the war from its cockpit. He gazed across the harbour at the battered collection of escort vessels, the two merchant ships at the wharf, their vital supplies already being unloaded. Was it enough? Two ships out of six. Would there be enough in them to keep Malta going until another convoy was organised?

As the harbour drew closer, the smell of smoke built, biting the back of Edmund's throat. Even with the light almost gone he could see the wrecks of bombed warehouses jutting like spines, all around the glow of fires not yet fully extinguished. Heavens above, the place was a ruin. And yet as the boat approached the wharf, he began to hear the sounds of the dock. The excitement in the voices of stevedores pushing out lighters to the transports, even some ragged cheers from knots of civilians. This place wasn't finished. Not by a long chalk. And whatever the future held, he wanted to be in the air protecting it. He'd do better next time. And the fifth kill could go hang. Didn't matter if he never got another one. They'd have to find someone else to plaster all over the papers. The papers...Edmund thought of Vickery, and decided not everything about the papers was so bad.

He'd thrown his whole life into the sea, gone in after it, and somehow come out again. In his head, he was already composing a letter to the journalist. Whatever words he eventually put down, the meaning would be the same. *You were right.* Edmund hoped he would see him again. The revelation was incandescent. He wanted to speak to Vickery again. To talk about poetry, and flying, and the weather, and nothing at all. A wish for the future. It was a gesture of optimism. He grasped it like a jewel.

The boat drew up to the jetty. As Edmund was about to step ashore, Carey produced a twenty-mil shell casing, and handed it to him. "A souvenir for you sir."

"Thank you." Edmund smiled awkwardly, slipped the scorched brass into his pocket. "And thanks for letting me at your gun. I think we did alright."

Carey chuckled politely. "Alright! I suppose that's one way of putting it, sir. Well, I'll be seeing you then - Ace."

"Yes, so long..." Edmund frowned at the poor joke, but Carey's face was sincere. "What do you mean, 'Ace'? I thought I told you-"

Carey grinned. "Well, you're on eight now sir. You can call yourself an ace, ain't that right? Even if you reckon you didn't earn some of those earlier ones."

"Eight? What are you talking about?"

The seaman pushed his cap back, scratched his forehead. "Well, those four Jerries you shot down."

"Four? What the blazes? I just blasted away. I suppose I may have hit one or two a bit, but..."

"You mean you don't know?" Carey's eyes were wide. "I watched you. You got two Stukas and two SM Seventy-Nines. Just you. Lots of other guns were shooting but I swear you're the one who knocked them down."

Could it be? Edmund blinked. Four more victories. Just like that. And this time he'd bloody well earned them. Think of it. No more idiotic pressure to get that fifth. No more glares and sneers from the other pilots. Eight! They would have to accept eight. And four of them shot down with a single gun from the pitching deck of a destroyer.

"I could confirm them for you sir, if that's what you're worried about." Carey turned his hat about in his hands like a steering wheel. "That's the word isn't it? Confirm?"

"Yes, that's right Carey." He breathed in and out, closed his eyes for a moment. As if it would stop now. And it didn't matter in the slightest. Not to him. The convoy had got through. Some of it. They had enough food, supplies, fuel to keep going a little longer. "The ship got them. They were *Hindscarth*'s kills. The starboard Oerlikon's, if you like."

Carey smiled, replaced his hat, saluted. "Right you are, sir. You're welcome at my gun any time you like."

Edmund returned the salute, climbed up the ladder onto the jetty, and was enveloped by the smoking, crashing, yelling cacophony of the port.

AUTHOR'S NOTE

'Harpoon' is a work of fiction, and the central characters are fictitious and not based on anyone living or dead. However, the details of the convoy Operation 'Harpoon' are based closely on genuine accounts, published and unpublished. These include Commander R. 'Mike' Crosley's 'They Gave Me A Seafire' (Crosley and his wingman 'Spike', Squadron Commander R.A. Brabner, and fighter controller 'Tricky' make appearances in the narrative) and the reports of senior officers of HMS *Argus*, *Eagle* and *Cairo* in the National Archives. HMS *Eagle* was a real aircraft carrier, though the Hunt-class destroyer HMS *Hindscarth* is entirely from my imagination. Some of the aerial combat was based on real events from WW2 and other conflicts, in particular Edmund's fourth kill being closely modelled on an incident from the Korean War, as recorded in 802 Squadron's line book and operations record book. I'd like to thank Frank Barnard, author of the WW2 flying novels Blue Man Falling, Band of Eagles, To Play The Fox and A Time For Heroes, for reading and commenting on the text, my long-time co-collaborator J.A. Ironside for doing the same, and Sharpe's Richard Foreman for his guidance and editing.

*

Printed in Great Britain
by Amazon

75405561R00066